M. WO

FATE

of

COINCIDENCE

Paperback: ISBN 978-0-578-34688-5
First paperback edition
December 2021

Edited by
Sharina Wunderlink

Cover art by
Baylorwood Publishing, LLC

Baylorwood Publishing, LLC.
El Cajon, CA 92020
www.baylorwood.com

Table of Contents

Dedication

This book is dedicated to those who want to give up. Persevere through the chaos. Stay true to yourself. You got this.

CHAPTER 1

Neesa

It was foreboding, a hand-addressed letter from her man, there against a book, like an assigned seating card. She dropped the mail she was holding onto the kitchen table and sat in the kitchen chair to open it. When was the last time he wrote her an actual letter? Two years ago, just before they went on a break. What would warrant a letter, that he could not say to her face?

She withdrew the two pages from the envelope and read the first line.

My sweetheart, it read.

A sentimental greeting, a terrible greeting, and she choked up. Was the relationship over, again? It had been six months since he called her *sweetheart*. Right before the breakup. To use it now meant something dire.

The second line confirmed, *you always wanted it straight, sweetheart, so I won't delay. I can't do this anymore.*

It's over. For good this time.

Neesa Ruse teared up and used the pages to fan her eyes; she could not read. She squeezed her eyes shut and wiped them with her free hand. Her throat ached. Heat rose throughout her body. Her emotions were in conflict, hurt and anger.

He had done it again. How could she be so stupid? She looked to the pages and read more.

This has nothing to do with you. Her eyes rolled in her head. *My journal will explain why I had to do it this way.* Her eyes rested on the book on the kitchen table.

2

She picked it up. She barely got through a few pages when she threw the book across the room, his journal to the floor.

She felt sick and needed air. Neesa ran outside. She was terrified. Her eyes darted up and down the street. She did not see his car anywhere. Was he on the run? Would she be next? Who was the man she had been with for these years? A monster. She leaned on her own car, back pressed against the passenger door. Then she slid to the ground.

Neesa fumbled in her pocket for a lighter, a cigarette and her phone. She lit the cigarette and sucked hard. The drag of harsh smoke cascaded down her throat filling her lungs.

She tried to dial 9-1-1 but her hands were sweaty, her body was shaking, she kept looking around in case he was going to jump out from somewhere. Just as she threw the lit cigarette, the call connected.

"9-1-1 operator, what is your emergency?"

The dispatcher heard a loud explosion on the other end of the line. The call went dead.

CHAPTER 2

Neesa

Six months later...

The young women rushed towards the exit, leaving the black lights, blaring music, sour sweat, cheap perfume, and warm beer behind. They tipped the night manager of the gentlemen's club as he handed them their California Express VIP cards. The women were thrilled as they walked out the building towards the outside bouncer. They had worked a day shift and left as soon as the 6 o'clock strippers arrived.

The bouncer grabbed their bags and escorted the young women to Neesa's car.

She popped the car trunk of her white Dodge Charger, and he hauled the heavy bags into it. The parking lot smelled of old car oil, asphalt, and piss. At a half past six, the pale waning crescent shone like a silvery hook in the night.

Sharp-eyed Neesa pointed to a dark dusty truck parked a few spaces from her car.

"Big Mike," Neesa said. "Whose truck is that?"

Big Mike shrugged. "Guy said he was a rideshare driver waiting to get a ping for his next pick-up," The bouncer responded. "I told him he had five minutes to leave this section of the parking lot."

"Einstein said time is relative," said Neesa.

"Where do you come up with this stuff," asked Tracey shaking her head at Neesa.

Big Mike looked at his watch. "Well, his time's up..."

As if on cue, the dusty dark truck backed out and headed towards the parking lot exit.

Neesa's muscles stiffened thinking about the dusty truck. The back bumper was caked with mud. She had been in numerous rideshare vehicles before and the vehicles were clean both inside and out. She also noticed the absence of a rideshare decal or light display. The hair on the back of her neck stood up.

The women each handed Big Mike a substantial wad of ones. Neesa added a couple twenties on top. He thanked the women, hugged them, opened the car doors, and waited for Neesa to pull out the parking lot. The sunroof was open, and the bouncer heard laughter and chatter as the two young women drove away.

After merging onto the interstate, Neesa pushed hard on the gas petal, getting the full force of the V8 engine. Her expression was tight and strained.

"Hey, Neesa.... earth to Neesa," called Tracey, a thick, young woman with shoulder length fire-red hair, accented with honey streaks. Her lace-fronts were always on point.

"Sorry, girl. Just daydreaming. You know how that is," said Neesa, apologetically.

"No, I don't," joked Tracey. "Hey, wanna go to the club tonight?"

"Sounds good," Neesa replied, not fully listening, her thoughts somewhere else.

"Ne-e-sa... Can you hear me?"

"Of course, I can," Neesa replied while checking her rearview mirror.

"So, what are you going to wear?" asked Tracey.

"I just might wear a tight ass dress."

"You, a dress?" "Tracey said. "Wow, showing some leg tonight. Get it girl! It's going to be a ladies' night, for sure."

"It's always ladies' night, we don't have boyfriends, remember," said Neesa laughing.

"I know that!" Tracey rolled her eyes. "Please stick with the dress, you never show your legs. Maybe we'll get some D tonight."

"You know how I feel about the burns on my legs." said Neesa. As if on cue, her scars began to tingle and itch. "Plus, I am perfectly fine without the problems that comes with the D."

"Girl, the lies you tell," teased Tracey.

"Where's the lie?" asked Neesa. Tracey pointed her finger at Neesa. They both laughed.

* * * * * * *

The entranceway of the liquor store chimed as the girls walked in, notifying the store clerk of their arrival. The store was small with about four rows in the center that was stocked of general items like household products, candy, chips, and cakes. Refrigerators lined two walls along the edge. One stored non-alcoholic drinks while the other held wine, spirits, and beer. The "good" liquor was lined on the wall behind the cashier.

Tracey went straight to the candy aisle, while Neesa opened a refrigerator to get bottled water with electrolytes. They both met up at the counter and looked behind the man standing at the register. There were at least a hundred different liquors to choose from. Neesa pointed and asked the cashier for a tall dark bottle. For some reason, she never remembered what the sizes were called; she was only concerned about type, the visual size, and the price. Tracey added a lighter and a pack of cigars to the purchase and Neesa added a pack of higher end cigars.

As the store clerk turned around to grab their pre-game drink, the entrance chimed again notifying the clerk of another person entering. Neesa turned to look at the new customer as he walked to the refrigerator and stared at the beer selection. She turned back to the store clerk but continued to keep tabs on the man at the back of the store by glancing up at the mirrors above the cashier.

The man walked towards them and stood too close to Tracey.

"Excuse you," Tracey exclaimed as she waved her hand in a motion to signal that he was in her personal space. He nodded and stayed right where he was. He had a peculiar smile. He licked his lips as they upturned into a smirk.

His bulging eyes washed up and down Neesa and Tracey's bodies. Tracey began to perspire; she was intrigued by the gall of the man. Goosebumps speckled Neesa's skin, her heartbeat slowly accelerated from unease.

The man stepped closer to the women and sat his beer on the counter.

"Would you get me a pack of ports while you're back there?" he asked the cashier.

"Excuse you," said Neesa. She slid the man's beer away from her stuff. "You can wait!"

His laugh caught her off guard. "Relax, baby girl," he said. Then he moved his eyes to Tracey. "Damn, you're cute. What's your name?"

Without hesitation, she batted her synthetic lashes and answered, "Tracey, but baby you can call me whatever you want."

Before Neesa knew it, her friend, and the rude man, who said his name was Charles, were exchanging social media names.

Neesa rolled her eyes and swiped her card to pay for her and Tracey's stuff. She nudged her friend, alerting her that it was time to leave the store. Neesa pointedly looked at her friend, trying to get her attention. Tracey briefly glanced back at Neesa, letting her know she was trying to end the chat with the dude.

"Damn, your body is banging," Neesa heard him say to Tracey.

"Thank you, I try," Tracey replied to him.

"Looks like someone feels left out," Charles said condescendingly to Neesa. "You're cute, too. Don't trip."

Neesa could not shake the uneasy feeling she had about him. He was just too assertive for her liking. As she pulled out of the parking lot, she noticed in her rearview mirror a truck pulling out of a parking spot a few spaces from the side of the building.

Neesa's phone chimed.

"I just sent half of what I owe you," said Tracey. "I'll get you back on the rest after work tomorrow."

"Okay cool," said Neesa as she refocused her attention to the road ahead of her. "Remember, poverty is slavery."

"Girl bye, with all that!"

"That dude in the store was an old head," Neesa flat out said to Tracey. "An old, outdated head."

"I thought he was alright," said Tracey.

"Yeah, you were quick to give him your number," said Neesa. "He looked old enough to be your uncle."

"Whatever. I gave him my profile name, not my phone number," Tracey said defensively. "As a matter of fact, I think you could have been nicer to him."

"Ha...no one told you to think," said Neesa. Her eyes moved to her rearview mirror. The blinding high beams of the vehicle behind them made her eyes squint. She scanned her surroundings and then refocused on the road. Turbulence stirred in her belly as a threatening feeling consumed her mind.

The women drove towards Tracey's house in silence. Since Tracey was accompanying her tonight, Neesa extended an olive branch by letting her co-pilot and pick the tunes. Tracey switched the radio, and heavy beats blared loudly through the car speakers. Deep bass flooded the car and thumped in their chests. Divine sanction graced their ears as the masterful words of California rappers provoked Tracey to gyrate in the front seat.

Neesa's mind's eye was encased with brooding thoughts which poached her psyche. Her mouth was drawn into a straight line. She started to bite her lip. She could not put her finger on what was occupying her mind.

Tracey turned and glared at Neesa.

"Hello!" Tracey shouted, pointing a finger out the window.

"Oh, my bad, girl." Neesa quicky turned the steering wheel sharply into Tracey's driveway. Neesa felt disturbed. She felt like she was mentally on autopilot. Time passed so quickly that she swore she was going through life in a highway hypnosis state.

"Woman, wake up," ordered Tracey. "If you keep spacing out like that you're going to get into an accident."

"I said I was sorry," Neesa snapped.

"I accept," Tracey said as she laughed at her friend. "So, do you want to head to the club around 10 tonight?"

"Sure, no problem," Neesa answered. "I'll call you when I'm on my way."

They waved to one another as Neesa drove off. Neesa noticed the high beams of the vehicle behind her were no longer in view. She tried to convince herself she was just being paranoid.

* * * * * * *

The music pumped hard through the speakers as they drove to the club later that night. They bobbed their heads and sang along to the lyrics. It was refreshing to get out and mingle. Neesa was around people all the time but something about the nightclub gave her permission to let loose. Maybe it was the fact that she could meet a guy she liked, at least for the night. Life was short.

"Hey girl, turn that song up," she told Tracey.

"What?" Tracey said in disbelief. "Did I hear you correctly?"

"Hey, tonight I just want to let loose."

"I hear that," agreed Tracey.

They both laughed and the bass pounded in their ear drums.

When they arrived at the club, they finished off a couple shots, in the car, of the brown liquor they brought earlier. The two young women walked straight to the front of the line, showed their V.I.P. cards and were waved through. They heard the annoyance of the angry people who were waiting in line. Neesa and Tracey never went anywhere that they had to stand in line for.

Inside was packed. The smell of liquor and sweat filled the air. The bass vibrated throughout their bodies.

"Okay," yelled Tracey. "My game plan, no short guys or gold teeth."

"You're silly," laughed Neesa. "Good luck."

As they made their way to the bar, someone caught Tracey's eye and she disappeared into the crowd. Neesa made her way to the bar and sat on a stool. She wanted to take in the scenery before jumping right in.

"Excuse me, can I buy you a drink?" asked a tall, dark sexy man.

"Sure, wine. Your pick," Neesa said with a flirtatious smile.

She did not expect to find someone so quickly. She watched as he ordered their

17

drinks. She took hers from the bartender and sipped it. He did as well. Red wine was one of her favorites.

"I'm Micah and you are?"

"Neesa," she said. "So, who are you here with?

"My brothers. You?"

"My girl, Tracey," Neesa said. She noticed he had a strange look on his face. "No, not like that. My friend. Hey, I'm strictly dickly."

"Woo. Thank god," he replied. "I thought I made a wrong turn."

They both laughed and chatted until they finished their drinks. She went to the restroom, and he walked her over to it. She felt hot and wet; this guy was turning her on. She was beginning to renege on what she told Tracey earlier about the D. The way he looked at her she knew they would have some fun later that night. When she got out, they looked at one another and like animals, began to kiss. It was nice and short but great at getting the juices flowing again. Then he took her hand and led her to the dance floor.

It was crowded but he smoothly found a way in. Micah was a good dancer. His body was hard, he felt good and Neesa was having a wonderful time. She noticed him look down at her legs. She kept dancing, pretending not to notice, then she spotted Tracey was kissing some guy whose attire hollered "Catdaddy." It looked like Tracey was having an enjoyable time.

Suddenly Neesa realized she was dancing without Micah. A woman had taken his arm and was whispering in his ear. The woman kept looking over at Neesa with a smirk on her face. Micah looked back and waved to her to join. Neesa realized she lost her catch, but she didn't care. Time to move to the next one. He never came.

On the way home Neesa and Tracey stopped at a drive-thru taco shop to answer the quell of rumbling in their stomachs as the alcohol haze faded out of their systems. Neesa pulled out of the drive-thru and parked in an empty stall. Silence was broken by the sound of their moist ravenous bites, oil and sour cream dripped down their chins.

"I don't know how you eat just leaves and nuts," Tracey said between bites.

"I eat more than leaves and nuts. See," Neesa picked an avocado out of her veggie burrito, held it up, and then popped it into her mouth, which was close to maximum capacity.

They both burst into laughter and chewed up burrito squirted out their mouths and specked the steering wheel and dashboard.

"Damnit!" said Neesa using a napkin to clean the barely noticeable mess. "We can finish eating when we get to our pads." Tracey took the cue and rewrapped her meal in the foil and paper it came in. Neesa pulled back onto the road.

"So, let's go out tomorrow too," suggested Tracey.

"Okay, I'm down," Neesa said. "But Ummm.... what's with the guy you were with tonight?"

"Did he look familiar to you?" asked Tracey.

"Nope, I didn't get a good look."

"Girl, you need to fix your eyes. We met him earlier, at the liquor store, remember?"

"You have to be kidding me," Neesa's eyes widened in disbelief. Her forehead wrinkled as angry heat rose up her neck.

Changing the subject, quickly, Tracey asked "What happened to the guy who had his tongue down your throat?"

"Nothing at all," Neesa replied, hiding her mild disappointment at how easily he had left her. Neesa then steered the questioning back to Tracey.

"You told him we were going to be at the club tonight?" accused Neesa.

"Heck no! He just happened to be there."

"He looked kind of rough," said Neesa.

21

"Just how I like my men!" Tracey snorted, softening the mood.

Without warning, Neesa's eyes became wet with irritation as impeding high beams hastily approached from the car behind them, briefly blinding Neesa as she looked in the rearview mirror.

"What the hell," she scowled, turning the steering wheel to avoid a collision. She swerved into the right lane as shrill honking blasted from the passing truck, which then veered into their lane, right in front of her, and braked hard. Neesa anticipated the move. Her foot stomped the brake as her right arm instinctively stretched out to protect Tracey from impact.

CHAPTER 3

Janice

Her head fell to her chest and spit slid down the side of her mouth. Several hours later, a startling thud signaled for her to open her weary eyes. She reluctantly lifted her head, opened her eyes, and looked around to get her bearings. She was in her room. Janice Wright looked to the side of the bed down to the floor and saw her journal, unbound, and sprawled open, the culprit of her awakening.

It had fallen to the floor when she dozed off last night reading her inscriptions. She looked at the clock, her guests were to arrive at nine o'clock, that gave her three quarters of an hour, which was sufficient time to write. Anxiously, she put one hand on her nightstand to steady herself and leaned over to pick the journal off the floor with the other hand. The petite muscles in her arms and back steadied Janice as she pushed herself back and sat upright.

She wrote feverishly without pause. A salty bead of sweat slid down her tight aged skin and landed on the stationary as it created a damp period, signifying the sentence's end. Her weathered bony fingers closed the leatherbound journal, placing it on her bedside table. She then pulled her robe on over her aging shoulders.

Janice was having difficulty deciding which way the story should go. Do the women die in the car accident? Does the driver of the truck continue with his deviousness? She had already composed an outline for how she wanted the story to flow. However, her characters hardly behaved, and were most times bent on going in directions she had not planned for. That nuance did not deter her from continuing with the story. She felt writing about her characters was a bit dull if she could predict their next move. The longer she worked with and fleshed out the characters, the more she noticed they would choose to say or do things Janice had not necessarily outlined.

Her bedroom room smelled of stale damp breath, rose water, and shea butter. The planked floor was cold; a shiver ran up her spine, tingling the crown of her head as she rose out of the bed. Her bare, cracked feet shuffled her towards the relentless rays that peeked through a slit between the drapes of the tall window. Flecks of forsaken paint found solace in the window's crevices of wilted wood, dirt, and spider silk. She looked out and noticed a vehicle pull onto her driveway.

The car paused at a wooden, yellow orange ombre sign that swung nimbly on a short chain-link that was attached to an outstretched post. The words Shamba Place were painted onto a background of silhouetted elephants and giraffes. Hastily, Janice changed into a red and yellow kaftan and went outside to greet her guests.

She waved and motioned the driver to park alongside the front of the house. A lovely tall dark stallion got out of a polished black sedan and walked around the car to open the passenger door for, what Janice would call, a clotheshorse.

"Welcome to Shamba Place," Janice said as she spread her arms to demonstrate the view around them." Both man and woman trailed their eyes to the patchy green hillside. Pampas speckled several places, and an old Moreton Bay fig tree was clawed into the dense soil. Micah remembered climbing a similar tree at a park as a child.

Cynthia looked around disturbed by the natural surroundings.

"This place looks—"

"C'mon Cynthia," Micah interrupted as he grabbed the hand of the clotheshorse and ushered her towards the older woman.

"...like trash," whispered Cynthia, as she begrudgingly walked towards the feeble looking plank steps. Janice pretended not to hear the unimaginative woman.

"Shouldn't they get our bags?" Cynthia yelled back at Micah, raising her voice to make sure the old woman heard her. She looked around for the hired help and saw none.

"You have a bag boy, don't you?"

"Cynthia, I got it! This isn't downtown," Micah yelled standing at the trunk of the car.

"No, shit!" she complained, wrapping her arms around herself as a chill crept up her spine.

"Just leave your belongings here," Janice said to Micah, purposely not addressing the clotheshorse. "Charles is out back. I'll have him bring them to your room."

Cynthia gave Micah an 'I told you so' look.

"Come on in," welcomed Janice.

Micah followed behind, balancing their luggage in his arm; his sculpted physique bulged underneath his white t-shirt. He had been here before, many years ago when he was younger, but the old woman did not seem to recognize him.

The steps meekly complained as Janice led the couple up the porch and into her bed and breakfast. She gave her guest a brief tour and noted the rules: No smoking. No loud noise. No mess.

"Show us to our room, already," Cynthia demanded with an exaggerated yawn.

"Where the hell are your manners?" Micah scolded her. "Don't talk to her like that."

Janice, unbothered by the clotheshorse, led the couple up the front staircase towards their room.

"Dinner is at seven every night. There are clean towels and sheets. My husband Jack is here to help if you need any maintenance done," Janice reiterated.

"I share Shamba with you while you are away from home." Janice nodded her head towards the scenery out the window.

"I know you'll have an exciting time," she said while speaking directly to Cynthia.

"I doubt it," chirped the younger woman.

With that, Janice pulled her Kaftan up to her knees, so not to trip, turned, and disappeared down the stairs. The trim of her kaftan dusted the floor.

She softly murmured, "Only a fool tests the depths of the water with both feet."

CHAPTER 4

Neesa

A metallic stench weighed down the mild breeze from the retched internals on the porch. Motion lights lit her path as she made her way to the front door. Neesa looked down and saw mucus, clotted blood, hair, and moist flesh. A feeling akin to spiders sliding down her back caused the breath in her throat to catch. Neesa quickly sidestepped and cursed.

She heard breathing and she turned toward the sound. A cat's meow tickled her ears and caused her to shiver. Her nerves were already shot after nearly colliding into the vehicle on the highway. After driving

Tracey, it was now a quarter past three in the morning. She was exhausted.

"Prissy!" Neesa exclaimed. The neighbor's cat was intent on leaving tiny body parts on the porch.

Willing herself not to add to the heave, she held her breath, stepped over the muck, and tried to key the front door lock. Light pressure from the effort pushed the door ajar. A solicitation in-between the sill floated down to her feet as the svelte feline rubbed itself on Neesa's ankle. She noticed neither, only focusing on the fact that the door was opened a crack.

Her heart pounded in her chest and her senses became acute as Neesa turned back and did a second scan of her front yard, no movement except the beating in her chest. Her clammy hands pushed the door open wider as she took a minuscule step inside and gave the front room a once over, twice.

Everything seemed in order. The red sofa was the center focus of her living room. There was a wooden coffee table placed in front of it that matched the two end tables on either side of the couch. A large television was bracketed to the wall across from the couch. The dining room was an extension of the living room, the dining table also matched her living room furniture. Various pieces of mail, papers, and whatever else she felt like tossing there saturated the table like scattered puzzle pieces.

The door being unlocked coupled with the long night she had with her friend Tracey, the day reaper finally caught up to her, causing her body to plead for slumber. Burning the candle at both ends was generally the way she navigated life, however after a day at work, a night of festivities, and a near car accident, she was starting to rethink her candle burning antics.

Neesa wearily remembered the mess at her doorstep, gathered cleaning supplies, and went outside to tend to the bloody remains. A post-card sized piece of paper laid next to the vile. Since it did not have any muck on it, she put the piece of paper in the crease of her arm pit and walked the mutilated gift from Prissy to the outside trash bin.

Back inside, Neesa tossed the orange solicitation on the dining table. She told herself she would check it out when she woke up and also made a mental note to clean off the table.

Thirty minutes later, a freshly showered Neesa sat on the edge of her queen-sized bed, her thick ebony curls in its satin bonnet. Tomorrow is a new day she thought, as she reached over to her nightstand and looked at the time on her cellphone, it was technically already tomorrow, almost time for the day to begin for other people. She rubbed shea butter on her weary feet and slid her slender toes into fluffy socks. Then she formally got in bed, naked except for the socks, and pulled the cool white sheets and a mauve weighted blanket over her smooth shapely body. She squeezed her thighs together; her soft hands caressed her plump breasts. Neesa's nipples tightened to erection as her breasts yearned to be in her warm wet mouth.

She closed her eyes and fell asleep.

She was startled awake from her slumber by a loud sound. Neesa tried to sit up but winced from the pain and weakness in her muscles. The clock read a quarter past ten in the morning. She felt lightheaded and briefly thought her cranial ache was due to her alcohol consumption from the previous night.

In her robe, she walked into her living room where a pungent smell prickled her sinuses causing her to sneeze. As she made her way to the kitchen her achy body was reluctant to follow her lead, then something in her peripheral caused her to look towards the kitchen window. A vehicle drove down the street and passed her house. Her labored awareness made her unsure if the vehicle was hurried or going at residential speed.

She held onto the sink as her legs and feet began to betray her. *What the hell*, Neesa thought. The odor was strong. She checked the burners. The unlit stove was turned on. Gas fumes were smothering her lungs. She turned the knobs to the off position and darted around her single level home, ignoring her aches and lack of breath, to open all the windows and let the fumes dissipate. She then walked to the front door.

The door was slightly open. Again.

Breathing heavy, her heart jumped to her throat as her hand went to her chest.

Someone was here.

She paced back and forth and raised her damp palm to her warm forehead as chilling thoughts coiled in her mind. She closed and locked the door and picked up her phone.

Dialing on her phone was such a robotic effort that instead of dialing 9-1-1, Neesa pressed the 'TALK' button and...

"Hey girl, what's up?" said her friend.

"Tracey? Oops, I didn't mean to call you, I just..."

"Yeah, you did. Your subconscious knew I was having an outfit dilemma," said Tracey. "So, should I wear a red halter top and jeans or a black mini dress?"

"Tracey! Listen to me!" yelled Neesa. "I was calling the police. I think someone was in my house and tried to kill me."

"No, way. Are you serious?" asked Tracey.

"Don't I sound like I am serious? I'll call you back," Neesa was about to hang up.

"Wait, you can't leave me hanging. Tell me what happened," Tracey said.

"Tracey, I will call you back!" Neesa ended the call and re-dialed.

"9-1-1, what is your emergency?", said the operator.

"Somebody tried to kill me, they broke into my house," Neesa began.

"Okay ma'am, what is your name?"

"Neesa!"

"Neesa, are you hurt?" asked the dispatcher.

"No, he turned on the gas in my house," said Neesa.

"Neesa, who turned the gas on?" asked the dispatcher.

"I don't know exactly!" she said loudly.

"Neesa, please try to be calm. Now, are you sure? Did you see anyone in your house?" asked the dispatcher.

"No... but I know he was here," said Neesa.

"Who is he?" asked the dispatcher. "What is his name?"

"I don't know, damnit," screamed Neesa. "Just send the police!"

"Ma'am first I need your addr..." Agitated, Neesa hung up the phone and tossed it on the table before the dispatcher could finish the sentence.

The phone immediately rang, startling her.

"Neesa, this is the emergency operator, I need your address so that I can send a unit to you."

"Never mind. forget it," she cursed and hung up the phone.

Her cell phone rang again. It was Tracey calling back. Neesa ignored the call.

She decided to put the incident behind her, for the moment. She would stay mindfully alert rather than dwell on unknowns.

After Neesa cleaned her house and ran some errands it was a quarter to six in the evening, which happened to be a perfect time to relax before going in to work that night. The easiest way for her to sink into sleep was to watch a show or two. She found a crime series on a tv app, set the sleep timer for one hour, and pressed the play button. The storyteller was a woman who did her own makeup while recounting gruesome and twisted crimes. The stories fed Neesa's fascination with the dark side of humanity, and she was able to get a few makeup tips at the same time. The true crime story was interesting and held Neesa's attention until it didn't, and she began to doze off.

Just below the surface of sleep, not fully submerged in its depths, she heard a muffled sound. Thinking it came from the show she was watching, she sunk back into the warm arms of sleep. The muffled sound became more pronounced. It was her cell phone ringing.

This time she answered the call.

"Hello," she said while stretching her neck side to side as she got up and walked out her stiff legs.

"Dang, woman! Did you forget to call me back?" Tracey asked.

"Nope. Earlier, when I hung up with 9-1-1, I didn't feel like talking to anyone."

"What the fuck?" said Tracey.

Neesa paused, then let out a breath before she spoke. "I'm going into work tonight."

"Seriously, what the hell? You promised that we were going out tonight."

"I didn't promise anything," Neesa said.

40

"C'mon, you are being lame," said Tracey.

"Sorry girl, I'm not the best partying person to be around anyway," said Neesa.

"You're so typical," said Tracey.

"What's that supposed to mean?" Neesa said.

"Nothing, forget it. Tracey blew out an exaggerated sigh. "So, what happened to you anyway?"

"I'll tell you about it later, and this time I do promise," said Neesa looking at the screen on her phone. It was half past six in the evening. "I have to go."

Just as Tracey was about the say something, Neesa ended the call, walked to the kitchen, and tossed her phone on the dining table where it surfed on discarded paper. Both paper and phone fell to the floor. Neesa winced and cursed hoping her carelessness did not damage her phone. She picked up both objects, placed the phone in her robe pocket and flipped over the paper to read the information. Last night when

41

Neesa had picked up the paper, she thought the solicitation was orange, however now, upon further review she noticed it had more of an ombre scheme. "Come Unwind your Mind" was written in bold font. The flyer read as an invitation to a retreat boasting of meditation, yoga, massages, and nature hikes, located in the foothills of Southern California. She turned it over seeing a white blank backside. She flipped it back over and looked at the address. It was about an hour drive from her home. The minimalism of the invite resonated with her. It hinted of tranquil sunsets which would temporarily warm the icy unease she felt within herself.

On a whim, she dialed the phone number on the flyer.

CHAPTER 5

Janice

A couple hours before dinner, Janice was sitting outside on the front porch in a weathered wicker chair. Her two guests had gone on a stroll to the lake. Beside her on a table sat a tall cup of sweet tea garnished with tangy lemon slices. She picked out a sliced lemon and sucked on it, her left eye winced closed from the tart juice. She spit the lemon seeds into a napkin and placed the fruit's skin on it. She then picked up her journal and jotted down some ideas she planned to expound on later. Janice heard the phone ring, placed her journal and pen down on the side table, and rushed into the house to answer the phone.

"Hello, Shamba Place," she answered.

"Hi, I am interested in the event you are having this weekend," said Neesa on the other line.

"Oh, I'm sorry," said Janice. "You must be calling for the folks up the road. People get our numbers mixed up all the time."

Neesa looked down at the flyer and read out the phone number to verify she dialed the right number.

"The number here ends in 2357, not 2351," said Janice.

She looked down at the flyer again and noticed a dried bit of something stuck near the number 1. She used the tip of her teal polished fingernail to scratch the gunk.

"Oh, wow, my bad. I read the numbers wrong," Neesa replied. "Thanks. I'll call the correct number this time," Neesa said with a polite laugh.

Before the call was disconnected Janice said, quickly, "I have a bed and breakfast not far from there. You are welcome to stay here."

"Ummm, well I was looking for more of a retreat type setting," said Neesa.

"It is much quieter here. A soft bed, your own room, hot running water and flushing toilets. And if you choose to go to their little shindig, it is only a few minutes' drive up the road," Janice said.

"You know, that sounds nice," said Neesa.

Janice gave her the information on booking a stay at Shamba Place and hung up the phone.

Neesa scribbled the information on the back side of the flyer. She planned to drive up to the ranch and attend the event after she got off work. She thought about calling the lady at the ranch back because she forgot to tell the lady her name but decided against it.

CHAPTER 6

Janice

After the phone call, Janice drove to the local store to buy lemons, seeds, and groceries for dinner. Upon leaving the store, she dug in one of her grocery bags and retrieved a bag of salty sunflower seeds. She popped a few in her mouth, sucking and cracking them with her thick tongue and dull teeth. She walked a few yards to the post office which was located on the other side of the town's old bar. The post office and bar were in weathered cabins, the former being a couple square yards larger, of the two. The post office was no bigger than a short school bus. Two men sat out in front of the old bar playing cards, as another man leaned against the logged walls and spat out a gooey ball of tobacco in salutation to Janice. As she walked by, Janice matched his gooey salute by spitting out her own concoction of moist salty cracked sunflower seed shells.

She popped a few more in her mouth. Her salt laden tongue tucked the seeds between her gum and cheek.

Mailboxes aligned the outer side and back walls of the post office. Twenty or so boxes lined the inside walls. Janice walked to the backside of the quaint building, retrieved her mail, tossed the junk in the trash bin located nearby, and then walked to the front of the post office. The reception area was big enough for only one person to fit comfortably. She stood at the door waiting for the patron inside to finish their business. The old lady inside had wiry white hair and she and her twin sister were known as the blood-and-bones of the town. Unfortunately, one sister had developed dementia, so locals tended to keep an eye on her as she went about the town. The pale old twin, the one with her wits still intact, walked out passed

Janice as though she did not notice the melanated sun-kissed woman.

A tall man appeared behind the glass window. He lifted the glass, ducked his head down, and greeted Janice.

"Good afternoon, Carl," said Janice.

"Well, hello yourself," said Carl with a large welcoming grin. "You got something for me?"

"No, nothing to mail today," she said. "I just wanted to say hello."

"I see there is another one of those events going on up near your place," Carl said.

"Yeah, I saw the campers and cars driving up past my property," Janice said with a frown. "Perpetrators."

Both laughed.

"Hopefully, the main road doesn't get messed up like last time.," Janice said with a little irritation in her voice. "It's dirt for Christ's sake. Not asphalt."

Janice rolled her eyes at the thought.

"Enough about those crazy fools," she said as she spat sunflower seed shells out the post office door. "I have to go. I have guests up at the house."

"Good day to you, Janice," Carl said. He mockingly saluted her.

Janice began to walk away but remembered something and turned around before he slid the glass window back down.

"Carl, you spend time at the pub, right?"

He turned red from embarrassment.

"Is it that obvious?" He put his hand to his mouth to smell his breath.

Janice laughed out loud.

"No fool. Have you seen Jack?"

"Nope...not in a long while," he said with relief. "Tell him to stop by. The fellas miss him," he said. The corners of his mouth turned upward as he held back a laugh. Jack had been gone for several months. The locals used to think he was just a homebody because he stopped going into town, however, as one month turned to two and no one saw him, it was obvious to them that he must have left her. They figured if she wanted to pretend, he was still around, who were they to stop her delusion.

Janice stood stiff, piercing him with her eyes. The walls of the quaint building seemed to pull inward for Carl.

Carl's neck became moist as claustrophobia dug into his psyche.

"Is everything alright, Janice?" he asked hoping the crazy lady would just leave.

"Absolutely," she said with her chin raised high. "I'll see you later." She hissed goodbye over her shoulder as she walked outside. Ducking her head and aiming for the side of the walkway, Janice spat the seeds that were still in her cheek. The mucous dropping resembled egg whites fresh from the shell—thick and snotty.

CHAPTER 7

Janice

Cynthia sat on the windowsill, looking out the window onto the grounds behind the house. She saw Janice nearly trip over what looked like nothing. Taking an exaggerated deep breath Cynthia inhaled deeply on her cigarette as it dangled between her over-glossed lips.

Micah was in the bathroom touching up his beard in the mirror. The door remained open.

"Damnit," Janice yelled from outside down on the porch as she nearly stepped in rodent droppings.

"Jack, Jack!" she yelled.

She quickened her pace to find her husband.

"That old woman is out there talking to herself," Cynthia said to Micah.

"She's probably talking to her husband," he said.

"Oh, the handyman," said Cynthia as she rolled her eyes. "Right! Why haven't I seen him yet?"

"I don't know," he shrugged. "Damn, you're nosey."

Cynthia flicked her hot, dry ash in Micah's direction.

"I'm what, huh," she said. "I knew I shouldn't have come up here. I'm bored."

Raised in the backcountry, Micah learned how to keep out of other people's business. News traveled fast in the backwoods, but people respected each other's privacy.

He was the oldest of three boys. Micah's mother had left them when they were young. It was right after her birthday. Micah and his brothers had put together the little money they had made from ranch chores and brought her a necklace with a green stone. Their dad said she ran off with another man. His tone let them know the conversation stopped there.

Their dad taught Micah and his brothers to work hard, respect women, even despite their mother's failures, and always mind their own damn business. Part of minding their business was no further questioning about their mother's whereabouts.

A few years later, when Micah became an adult, he tried searching for his mother. His researched found several unsolved disappearances of women around the time his mom left. He never found her.

Micah kicked the bathroom door shut. White paint flakes fell to the floor. Cynthia remained unconcerned about his annoyance as she continued peeping at Janice talking to a shrub. The green foliage blocked her view of whoever Janice was pointing at.

Outside, Janice yelled again for her husband before finding him sitting behind a bush with a rake and pile of leaves nearby.

"What the hell," she pointed at the leaves. "Work won't get done by itself. Get the hell up!"

Her head raised up; eyes fix half a foot above her own.

"I need you to pick up the turds at the back door," said Janice.

She did not wait for an affirmative response from him.

"Where have you been by the way? I was looking for you yesterday."

She saw him shrug his broad shoulders.

"What's with you, Jack?" asked Janice. "Cat got your tongue?"

Again, not waiting for his response, Janice continued. "Did you see my new house guests, the lanky clotheshorse and scrumptious stallion?"

She heard him mumble something inaudible. Waving her hand to dismiss whatever it was, Janice started to walk back to the house, but turned back to her husband.

"Make sure to clean the porch out back, too!" she said. She began to walk off, then turned back around once more.

"Jack, what have you been up to lately anyway?" Janice asked and then speaking before he could answer, "Oh, that's right you said you been parlaying at the bar lately."

She saw him nod in agreement.

Janice rolled her eyes and walked toward her truck to get some things she had left in it from earlier. *Lying ass*, she said to herself. The postman had implied that he had not seen Jack at the bar lately.

Janice looked up to the house and saw Cynthia's prying eyes glaring down at her out the window. "For heaven's sake!" She rushed to the house, straight up the stairs, and gave the guest room door a hearty knock.

Micah answered it while using a towel to wipe the shaving cream from his face.

"Ma'am, something wrong?" he asked.

Janice pushed through the door and headed straight for Cynthia.

"Didn't I say no smoking!" the old woman yelled. "What's the matter with you?"

"What's the matter with you!" Cynthia said back.

"Cynthia, what did I tell you," Micah said looking at her as he got in between the two heated women. He apologized and told Janice it would not happen again.

The old woman stepped back, setting her eyes deep at Cynthia, turned, and left the room.

The sound of the young couple arguing filled the narrow hallway.

"What the hell is her problem?" Cynthia huffed.

Janice walked down the wood-trimmed hallway to her bedroom and sat in

an oak high-backed chair. She took her
journal out of her large pocket, opened it up,
and her pen began its dance across the pages.

CHAPTER 8

Neesa

At a quarter to seven, Neesa decided it was time to get ready for work. As she walked to her car to get her makeup bag out of the trunk, she took a deep breath of the clean fumeless air. The air felt nice and cool. She realized just how stuffy it was in her house. After getting her makeup out of her work bag, she went back inside.

Neesa took a bath, did her makeup, and left for work.

Tracey's house was on the way to the strip club. She decided to stop by and apologize for being short with her earlier.

Listening intently to the news on the radio, she did not notice the dark truck that followed close behind.

Neesa pulled up to her friend's driveway, but then changed her mind.

She will just try to convince me to go to the club for another ladies' night out.

Neesa pulled away and headed for work.

* * * * * * *

Up in the DJ booth, Neesa picked her music for her next stage set. She was dressed and ready. DJ Chaz sat back in his chair and turned to her as she told him about what happened earlier that day.

"Yeah, I think someone's after me or something."

"So, what happened, someone tried to gas you?" Chaz asked. "Who do you think it was?"

"I'm not sure," Neesa replied.

"I'll follow you home to make sure you get there safely if you want," offered Chaz.

"Yeah, thanks, that's cool," said Neesa.

Chaz was a nice guy, always looking out for her, but she only liked him as a friend. He had hinted that he would be up for a higher ranking if she were willing to give him a chance.

He was one of the first people she had met when she moved to this city six months ago. Their first encounter was at a carwash as they both were towel drying their vehicles. His truck was huge, gleaming and rims were on point.

They had some small talk; him being the initiator. He had told her he was a DJ at a strip club and since she was looking for a job, suggested Neesa came in and auditioned. She took his offer.

He was cute, not necessarily her type though. He had shiny dark long hair, shaved on the sides, which was usually worn up in a rubber band.

Several dancers at the club vied for his attention due to his sex appeal and infectious personality. Unfortunately for them his assumed flirtations were just a DJ being affable to secure the tips at the end of the night. His allure often confused his stilettoed followers. He had been in the entertainment business for a long while and knew how to expertly skirt unwanted attention.

Many of the guys who worked in the strip club thought they were the shit because they had beautiful women around them. It was just part of the job though. Geeks in real life felt like kings when they came to work. Pussy everywhere; a dream come true. Chaz carried himself differently.

Neesa looked at the girl on stage and turned back to Chaz who was turning knobs on the mixer and keying the computer.

"Am I next?" Neesa asked.

"Yep. After this song," he said.

"I can't believe I'm still doing this," she confessed.

"You and me both," he said.

They laughed as Neesa headed back down the stairs from the DJ tower. She sat on a purple velvet couch and reminisced about her first time on stage, auditioning. She remembered the awkwardness and embarrassment.

A voice on the loudspeaker announced her name to go to the stage to pole dance for the first time in her life. She walked slowly to keep her balance in the five-inch clear stiletto heels while trying to look sexy at the same time. The music started and a jazzy vocalist sang through the CD from the DJ equipment. Neesa felt sweat trickle out of her pores.

Everyone in the room seemed to have come to a complete standstill. All eyes were on her, the then new girl. The new girl with burns on her legs.

Four ladies sitting at the bar focused on her. There was a neon pink and blue light above them with the club's name on it, "Kitty Cat Gentlemen's Club." The ladies were wearing the typical stripper attire: fishnet stockings, lace, and leather lingerie. The bar was the standard version of a wood countertop and ten bar stools. Behind it was a glass mirror with a full selection of all the cheap beer and wine a person could think of. Half-drunk beer mugs and shot glasses separated the bar patrons from the server.

She saw the strippers pointing at her and laughing.

There were nine men in the audience (two of which were the manager and bouncer). The other seven men were scattered about the room. None of them seemed to know one another. One customer was sitting up front and center of the stage. He was wearing a cream-colored shirt that was unsuccessfully trying to cover a huge beer belly. His khaki pants matched the shirt, somewhat dingy. The man's face looked scruffy, with white-peppered hair that made up his five o'clock shadow. The hair on his head was a mess of curls and waves that used to be black but now complemented his facial hair. The man leaned forward and smiled at Neesa, never taking his eyes off her.

66

She moved toward the pole at the center of the stage. She danced swaying her hips from side to side while keeping a hold of the pole like a child holding its mother's hand.

As the first song ended, Neesa reached behind her back and fumbled like a virgin boy trying to unclasp his girlfriend's bra for the first time.

Another R&B song played and Neesa got down on the floor and crawled slowly like a cat in heat towards the man sitting in the front of the stage. He leaned back in his purple velvet chair. Neesa thought of the sexy panties she had on, shaped like a butterfly and crotchless. She felt moist, from the nervousness. She stood up again and took one leg out of her panties at a time. Then she realized she was too far from the pole. She almost lost her balance and was flushed with embarrassment.

When the song completed, the DJ announced, "And that was the lovely Jezebel!" He drew out her name as only a DJ could.

Neesa got the job and for her first night, she brought home one hundred forty-nine dollars. She was so thrilled with herself. She was finally getting control of her life again.

Chaz announced Neesa which snapped her out of her trance. "Jezebel to the stage!"

Neesa jumped up and cursed. These days she wore thigh-high boots to cover her burns.

As she danced, the only men in the club played pool. Some girls were at the bar giggling loudly and guzzling drinks while some of the other ladies walked drunkenly toward the guys at the pool table.

* * * * * * * *

Later that night after her shift Neesa tipped and waved goodbye to the doorman as she and Chaz walked to their cars.

Chaz's phone rang.

"What's up? Alright! Yeah," Chaz said into his cellphone. He turned his head to look back at the club entrance. The other bouncer was waving him to come back inside.

"He did what?" asked Chaz. "I'm coming right now."

He told Neesa the club manager, Billy, needed him to go back inside to handle a drunk customer.

"No worries. Go ahead. I'll be fine," said Neesa. She hugged herself as a chill ran up her spine.

"I'm sorry but I promise I'll make it up to you," he said. "Text me when you get home, so I know you got there safely."

They hugged one another goodnight.

On the way home, Neesa decided to stop by Tracey's house once again. The lights were on inside. Her knocks on the front door were drowned out by loud music, so she tried the doorknob. It was unlocked and she entered. It smelled of warm beer, cheap perfume, and weed.

Tracey was drunk and was waving her plastic martini glass in the air in a salute to the new arrival.

"Hey, look who decided to show up," slurred Tracey.

"What up," said Neesa. "You didn't miss anything tonight. Work was pathetic."

Tracey rolled her eyes and walked to the kitchen. Neesa followed behind but Tracey turned around looking surprised.

"You're still here?" she said.

There were a few people in the kitchen, fixing their last drinks and smoking blunts. A few more were getting out of the hot tub in the backyard.

Tracey put her hand on Neesa's shoulder and nudged her towards the front door. Neesa grabbed Tracey's hand and yanked it off her.

"What the hell!?" said Neesa. "Don't put your hands on me."

"Yeah, so it was nice of you to come, but everyone is leaving now," said Tracey.

"You know what?" said Neesa. She had planned to apologize and invite Tracey to go with her to the yoga retreat.

"Forget it," Neesa stormed out, agitated. She heard Tracey yell at the other stragglers to leave. They followed Neesa out the door.

"I told you I have a date!" Tracey slurred loudly.

A voice laughed at her and said, "Yeah, more like a booty call."

Unaware of the truck parked down the street, Neesa sat in her car infuriated. She put the keys in the ignition and watched as people left Tracey's. Then she took the keys back out of the car ignition, opened her car door, but shut it again, hesitant. She was in no mood to confront a drunk Tracey. Neesa felt like she could knock Tracey out. She used her better judgment and drove off, still unaware of the truck that pulled up to Tracey's house. If she had stayed a while longer, Neesa would have seen a familiar face make its way up the walkway, play with the now locked door, and walk-in.

CHAPTER 9

Tracey

He stepped inside, it smelled like beer, bud, and warmed scented wax. He blinked his eyes to quickly adjust them to the dark entryway and held his breath as he slowly closed the front door. The locking mechanism made a clunking sound as metal hit metal.

Tracey thought she heard something and sat up from her bath, trying to focus her hearing to the sound.

"Hello?" she said. She heard nothing and sank back into the peach fragrant bubbles.

He was inside in the living room, his heart pounding in his chest. There was no sight of her, but he heard her voice. His palms were sweaty. His eyes now adjusted; he made his way through the living room to the hall to see where she was. Candlelight shadows danced out of what he assumed was a bathroom. He then turned back towards the living room hitting his knee on a plastic chair and stepping on a discarded red cup making it crunch underneath his boot.

He held his breath and kept still.

Water slushed around the tub and some seeped to the floor. She loved the way the silk blanket of bubbles felt as they floated along her skin. Trying to sober up some, she picked up a glass of water near the tub and chugged it down.

She had a visitor coming, someone Neesa would not approve of. She was trying to listen out for the knock on the door announcing his arrival. Tracey figured he would text her if he were waiting outside. She looked around for her phone and did not see it.

"Damnit."

She hoped he would make it; it had been a minute since she had a real man in her bed.

There was another sound.

"Babe is that you?" Tracey asked.

"Of course, it is, sweetie," he said forcing a joking tone to his voice. Why? Were you expecting someone else?"

"Oh snap," she said. "How did you get in?"

"The door was open, so I let myself in."

Tracey was sure she had locked the door after the last guest had left.

"Come in here and let me see you," he said.

"I'm in the tub, let me rinse off first." She was a little peeved at how he just walked into her place. Unease settled within her body and despite the hot water running over her, as she stood up and showered to rinse off, her skin prickled with chills.

He sat down on the black velvety couch with his arms spread and legs wide open.

Tracey came out the bathroom in only a towel. Her bare feet padded on the hard floor as she walked down the hall to the living room where the man sat in waiting. She came toward him dropping her towel seductively in the process. He grabbed her body and yanked her close, causing her to knock her phone off the glass coffee table. She began to tense up. He was moving fast, and his hands grabbed her breasts, squeezed, and tugged hard. He was hurting her.

"Damn. Take it easy,' she said, trying to pull away.

"Shut up!" he said. His force and tone took her by surprise.

"Who the fuck are you talking to?" The strength in her voice wavered a bit.

He let go and stood up to tower over her. His hands were weathered, wrinkled, and strong. Stronger than she anticipated for someone of his stature. In the same motion, he pushed her onto the couch. Tears began to form in Tracey's eyes, she sniffed trying to keep them at bay. He pushed her face into the back of the couch, unzipped his pants, and proceeded to take what he came for. She screamed in pain as his meat stretched her, causing her to bleed.

He yanked Tracey's head up by her hair and slammed it back into the couch pillows cutting off all her air. She became motionless.

His breaths became more rapid and deep.

"Isn't this what you wanted?" he said.

He noticed she was not moving but kept going until he was finished. He got off and turned her around. At that moment, Tracey kicked him hard in his junk, stunning him for a split second. It was her chance to run for the front door. She had to think clear. She had to get away.

"Get over here bitch!" he yelled. He snatched Tracey back towards him causing her to crash onto the glass table.

"Why are you doing this?" she pleaded.

Glass shards pierced her skin. Everything was happening so fast. Was he just playing around? She was not sure. She did not know him enough to know whether this was a game or not. Her intuition leaned toward *no games being played*. Her head was pounding from booze and the craziness that was her current situation. He put his dry hands around her neck and squeezed hard, just as she managed to stretch out her arm through broken glass and press a button on her phone. It was the speed dial number for Neesa.

* * * * * * * *

Neesa, still upset, looked at her phone display which read an incoming call from Tracey. She tossed her phone on the passenger seat.

The phone rang; unanswered.

CHAPTER 10

Neesa

Neesa woke up a little after ten in the morning, which was early for those in the industry. She slipped her cold feet into red fuzzy slippers and wrapped herself into a white fleece robe. She set the coffee maker, went to the bathroom, brushed her teeth with charcoal coconut oil toothpaste, and washed her face. She felt anxious and unsettled for a reason she could not put her finger on. She then went back to the kitchen and made an egg sandwich. She ate the sandwich and sipped coffee from her mug while looking out her window.

Afterward, she dropped some mail off at the post office and spent most of the day running a few errands.

Neesa decided to go work a few hours at the club. She liked how during day shifts, the customers came in, ate free pizza and burgers, watched the naked women on stage, and then got lap dances. They did not pussyfoot around. The daytime regulars were on a time limit. Typically, they only had an hour lunch break. Making money was straightforward. The drawback was sometimes there were not enough customers to go around.

At about 4pm, her shift was over. Neesa pulled her phone out of her bag, a missed call notification from Tracey still sat at the top of her screen. She called Tracey back, but the call went straight to voicemail. She did not like showing up anywhere unannounced, however, something in her gut told her to go and check in on her friend. She also wondered, who Tracey had invited to her house the night before.

Neesa pulled up to Tracey's house. It was quiet, no music or television sounds. She figured Tracey was passed out from her previous night's drinking binge. Neesa knocked. No answer. She tried turning the door handle, something sticky transferred to her hand. She could not tell what it was, but it had a familiar smell. The door was unlocked, and before going in she called out to her friend.

"Tracey," she called. No one answered.

Feeling like one of those idiot women in movies, she slowly pushed open the front door.

"Tracey? Hey girl...you awake?"

A metallic stench disturbed her breathing. An eerie feeling of wrongfulness loomed in the air. She did not have to go far to find out why. Laying naked atop broken glass was Tracey. Her body had a greyish tint. Her eyes were open staring directly at Neesa. She saw Tracey's hand clinched to her own cellphone.

Heat rose up Neesa's body and she rushed out of the house screaming. Her abdominal muscles contracted and the pressure within intensified. A burning sensation grew in her throat and bile rushed up. Vomit pushed between her lips. She could barely breathe as her heart drummed in her chest. She wiped her mouth and tried to calm her breathing. Neesa fumbled for her cell phone and dialed 9-1-1.

"9-1-1 Operator...what is your emergency," said the voice on the other end of the phone.

"My friend is dead! Please hurry!" she said through tears.

"Ma'am please calm down," said the operator. "Who's dead?"

"Just get the police! 555 Miranda Drive," yelled Neesa as she hung up the phone and dropped to her knees.

The police and paramedics arrived. A tall muscular Black woman detective walked onto the crime scene, under the police tape, to talk to a group of first responders. The detective asked Neesa questions.

Tell me what happened? What did you do before the murder? How long did

*you know Tracey? Did you see anyone
suspicious lurking around? Why did you
come here today?*

The voice of the detective was dulled
by the rush of blood coursing in her head.
She shook her head side to side. Her throat
tightened and her voice was thick. She
answered the questions the best she could.
Ultimately, not providing sufficient
information. The detective placed a business
card in Neesa's hand and let the grieving
woman leave.

Banging on the steering wheel with
her fists, Neesa felt Tracey's death was
somehow linked to her own house being
gassed. She blinked rapidly to clear the tears.
*I should have answered her call! Fuck, fuck,
fuck!* Her face was wet with tears. It felt as
though wind was knocked out of her and she
could hardly breathe.

She managed to drive herself home
and shower. As she sat on her bed in her
robe, she knew she had to let people know
what happened to Tracey. She knew staying
at home right now would keep her
questioning and blaming herself.

Neesa decided to go back to the strip club and work a nightshift to keep her mind occupied. Death was common in her line of work. Many dancers overdosed on drugs, committed suicide, and had heart attacks before the age of 25. Her feelings wavered due to an abundance of unfortunate circumstances. She was sad, confused, and angry.

Neesa got dressed, texted one of her regulars to come in and see her, and she headed to work for the second time that day.

CHAPTER 11

Neesa

Her regular, Matt, showed up, with flowers. He seemed like such a quiet little man, clean-cut, pale. Jezebel was guaranteed five hundred dollars for a couple hours of ego stroking and domination.

Neesa put on a black stripper bikini and a long black sheer robe. She held a riveted leather feather whip in one hand and walked out of the dressing room. The little pale man was one of the weird ones.

"Hi doll," he said, leaning over to kiss her cheek and handing her the flowers.

Neesa responded dryly and sat the flowers on the bar.

He paid for the VIP section. In character as Jezebel, Neesa asked the pale man questions that involved him talking about himself.

"How was your day, Matt?" she said.

"It was glorious. Two of my projects came through. I made a ton of money on a stock I have had for a year now. Oh, and my wife is out of town visiting her sister, so I have peace and quiet for a couple days."

He smiled, then frowned.

"Jezebel, am I a bad man for coming here behind her back? I mean, I asked her to do things, but she just won't. She said she is repulsed by me whenever I mention sex games."

"Matt, I will make you feel better," Neesa said. "I love the games we play together." She winked at him, and he rubbed his man-piece.

Men were self-absorbed, especially the ones who came into strip clubs. They believed strippers were their therapists and girlfriends.

The waitress brought their drinks, a whiskey with no ice, an extra empty glass, and a bottled water for Jezebel.

"Can I get you all anything else?"

"Yeah, some privacy," said Matt. Jezebel hit him across the shoulder with her whip.

"Do not talk to her that way!" she said. "Apologize now and tip her!"

He did as he was told. Jezebel and the waitress nodded to one another as the waitress left.

Matt poured half the whiskey into the empty glass and then sat it on the side table. He then held it up to her dark red lips. She sucked on her inner cheeks causing her mouth to fill with moisture as she leaned closer to the rim of the whiskey, parted her lips, and let warm spittle slide into his glass.

"Baby, dance for me," he said.

"What did you say?!"

"I'm sorry, Jezebel. I mean…," his eyes looked to the floor. "…would you please dance for me?"

He then looked up at her and began to stroke himself with his free hand, she smacked him across the face with the whip. He stopped stroking and looked at her with glossy eyes. His look brought her thoughts back to Tracey the previous night, how she looked so drunk.

"Put the drink down," she said shaking the image from her head.

"Can I have a sip, please," he asked but did as he was told. She said nothing as she pushed him further back in the couch with the aid of the ball of her stiletto boot pressed firm on his little package. She turned around and began to sway her hips side to side. All he could see was her round peach. She began to rub her hands all over her body and backed up towards him.

Matt leaned forward and sniffed Jezebel. She turned around and pushed him back into the couch again. She wished she could punch the person who murdered Tracey.

"Pick up the drink," she said.

He did as he was told and held the glass up to her. A thick mucus loggie slid out her mouth into the whiskey. He was panting, his eyes were glazed, he was ready. She stood back and stared at him. Just like a track runner waits for the gun shot, he was back to the edge of his seat.

"You may drink," she said.

He slurped down the drink with the cocktail straw. The front of his pants darkened from his wet discharge.

She wondered if the person who murdered Tracey had left similar evidence behind.

One beverage down and one to go.

Jezebel opened her water bottle and took a long drink. The man began to aggressively stroke himself again.

"Stop it!" she commanded and ordered him to the floor on all fours like a dog. The crack of his hairy butt was on display. He looked pathetic, weak, and energized. She picked up the second glass of whiskey, took out the cocktail straw, and sat the drink on the floor about a foot from his face.

"Oh, my goddess, yes," he whispered. She squatted down in front of it, like the Lil Kim album cover, and pulled her thin panties to the side.

He watched her attentively, he started panting again, drool slid down his mouth waiting for her next command. She inched closer to him. He could smell her sweetness as she positioned the whiskey underneath her. She released. Warm urine drizzled out of her, into the glass. Matt was salivating as he watched the wet flow enter his beverage.

She stood up and patted herself dry with a napkin. He stayed on all fours and waited. She placed the straw in the drink. Matt began to erect; he knew it was time.

She pointed her whipped to the drink and nodded in affirmation.

He sipped and savored the warm urine whiskey. Air sucking sounds came from below as he tried to suck up every drop.

"Get up," she said. He did and sat back on the couch. His face was wet with perspiration.

He got what he wanted, and it was time for him to leave.

Matt paid her, walked stiffly to the men's room, cleaned up, and left the club. Easy money for her. $500 normally brought a smile to her face, however, the image of Tracey's body lying in glass was burned into her mind.

She went to the dressing room and showered. The strip club was the only "premier gentlemen's club" in the county, equipped with new showers, chefs, and a gym.

Neesa sensed, from their sneers, that some of the ladies in the dressing room were salty because they knew she had just made bank.

Around midnight, Neesa decided it was time for her to go home. She was glad she came into work to keep her mind off her murdered friend. One of the girls tried chumming up to her as she got dressed.

"Wow...that is so sad, girl. So many girls kill themselves in this business," said a stripper named Sonja.

"She didn't kill herself!" Neesa said. "Tracey was murdered!"

"My bad girl. I just thought...I mean you know how Tracey liked to party," said Sonja as she backed away from Neesa.

The shock and denial of what happened was fading away, only to be replaced with guilt and anger.

"You are so fucking stupid," Neesa said to the boy-bodied stripper.

"My bad, no need for the attitude" said Sonja under her breath as she walked away. "Damn bitch has problems."

Neesa heard every word and as benign as they were, the words pulled the trigger and her suppressed anguish rose. She kicked off her boots sending them onto the floor with a loud thud and hopped off her stool. She used one hand to grab Sonja's neck and the other cocked to deliver a deserving blow. Then she hesitated. This was not the way to fix her solemn dejection.

Chaz walked into the dressing room just in time and lifted Neesa by the waist.

"What the hell?" said Chaz. "Calm down."

Neesa wiggled free of his grasp. She did need to calm down. The chick was only trying to give sympathy.

Chaz let her go. The other girls in the dressing room gathered to see what they had missed. Neesa grabbed her stripper gear and shoved them into her bag.

"I'm out," she said as she pushed passed Chaz towards the exit.

Chaz followed and walked Neesa out to her car.

'I don't understand why this happened," Neesa said to him. "Who would want to hurt her?" Snot began to swell within her nostrils and tears marked by black mascara running down her cheeks began to flow. Her eyes stung as she wiped them with her hands.

"You're tripping...go home and rest. I'll call you later to check on you," said Chaz.

She handed him his tip. He put his hand up in refusal.

He watched her drive away.

Neesa was exhausted as she pulled into the gas station mini mart. She went inside. The lady behind the register recognized her. They both greeted one another. It was almost one in the morning. She was tired and needed something to keep her awake. She made her way to the aroma of hot coffee brewing. There were a couple of reasons why she always went to this gas station on the way home from work. One, it was open 24 hours. Two, the coffee was always fresh.

Neesa heard the door chime ring as someone else walked in. The lady behind the register greeted that person as well. It was unusual for anyone else to be there at that time of night. Neesa knew people came to the store at all times of the day, but she felt safer knowing she was the only customer there at that late hour. She turned to see who had come in. She imagined a rough-looking trucker or even some young kids who were driving home after late-night partying.

An older transient woman walked towards her. Seeing older people out late at night was rare. Neesa was too tired to care.

She just wanted to get home.

CHAPTER 12

Neesa

After running in to get a quick coffee at the 24/7 mini mart, Neesa veered right and entered the freeway going south. It was a foggy night. She had to keep her eyes focused on the reflectors on the road lines to stay in her lane. Her Dodge headlights turned the fog into a white fleece blanket blocking her vision.

A military base surrounded both sides of the freeway. As she merged onto the loop for the state route going east, she noticed the vehicle behind her doing the same. That time of the night the roads were sparse, especially eastbound. She was thankful her car had a ton of power because the freeway took a steep incline through the hills.

The radio was tuned to her favorite paranormal station. One of her girls at work had put her on to the station when Neesa had given her a ride home after a tiresome night of dancing. A woman called in to the program to share an experience she had encountered.

"I walked in on a cat funeral," said the woman caller.

"One of my four cats died, and I placed it on the bed in my guest bedroom," *she went on. "When I came back to the room, I noticed the temperature had dropped. It was colder in there and my three other cats were all around him. They didn't even notice I was standing there."*

Neesa's sadness grew deeper.

The white fog thickened as she made the decline. Vehicle lights were fast approaching behind her but the vehicle itself was concealed by the thick fog. She strained to see beyond the white glowing substance in front of her. Suddenly there was a clear patch in the fog as the freeway began to level out.

The lights of the vehicle behind her kept approaching fast and were in her lane. *Highway patrol?* If it was not law enforcement, then Neesa thought the driver may have fallen asleep. She switched from the middle lane to the far-right lane. At the last moment, the other vehicle swerved and sped past her down the freeway. She yelled as she flashed her high beams on and off. She was exasperated. She exhaled, not realizing she had been holding her breath the whole time and continued listening to the radio show.

The rear lights of the vehicle ahead quickly disappeared in the dense fog. The radio show host was talking to the woman cat caller about her experience. The host, Trent Coast, asked the cat lady if she practiced magic. She did. She told him that often when she practiced spell work, her cats would immediately rush in the room when she began to do her work. Trent told her that witches often report that their cats arrive on the scene once spellcasting commenced, however, it only happened when positive magic was involved.

Neesa wondered what came in when negative energy was involved.

She passed a vehicle on the side of the road and sent good vibes to whomever it was. These days people had cellphones to get help with emergencies. Hopefully, they had good phone reception. Sometimes through the hills, when she was on a phone call as she reached the small peak, her cellphone lost reception until the decline.

The vibes must have worked because she saw the vehicle in her rearview mirror pull back onto the freeway. She wound down the window, the chilly air stiffened her skin and goosebumps perked up. Tears filled her eyes. She blinked them away as she checked her rear mirror. Another car was speeding and was on her tail. Her hands gripped the steering wheel tight. Her eyes were hyper focused, trying to see through the fog ahead. She was sick of cars bullying the roads, but she had no fight in her tonight.

Neesa swerved into the far-left lane to avoid getting hit from behind. The truck did the same and she heard its engine rev as it closed the distance between them. Neesa swerved back to the middle lane, but it was too late. The truck rammed her left back bumper sending her vehicle spinning as it screeched off the junction that merged down to a street below. The Dodge tumbled a few hundred feet.

Neesa was alive but pinned in. She managed to use her hands to feel for the seat belt buckle. It loosened from her body. Her dash clock read a quarter to one. She wriggled her legs and winced as sharp metal cut deep into her shins. Her neck ached which made it difficult to keep her head up. Her ribs felt crushed. Blood had blurred her vision. She knew she had to get away from the vehicle. She made a failed attempt to stand on her injured leg and fell back to the ground. Glass pierced her bruised flesh as she tried to escape on her belly. She could taste the metallic crimson running down her face. She used her arm to wipe warm blood out of her eyes. Neesa collapsed on her back.

When she looked up at the cement ramp above, she noticed a figure watching her.

Choking on blood, she cried out for help. She grew cold.

Twenty minutes later, emergency lights flashed. Neesa was rushed to the hospital.

Bright red splotches turned to a deep purple all over her body. Her arms and legs felt weighted down. Her head was wrapped in a cloth bandage. She ran her dry tongue over her lips and cut her tongue on a cracked tooth. She was shaken up but luckily without any broken bones. She heard the doctors' converse about how lucky she was. They asked Neesa about her next of kin. Without giving a response, she softly settled back to sleep.

When she woke up in the middle of the night a nurse was standing over her.

"You are one lucky lady," said the nurse. "Someone sure is looking over you."

"What happened," asked Neesa. She knew about the accident, but she wanted to know the details of her injuries. The nurse gave her a rundown of the night.

"When can I go home?" asked Neesa.

"You should rest," said the nurse. "The doctor is doing his rounds. He'll be here in a few minutes."

Neesa was released from the hospital at 5 a.m. It was either that or she was walking out, period. She was warned of her injuries and given a bottle of pain pills. The hospital called a rideshare to drive her home at her request. She was not in the mood for people and just wanted to go home, clear her head, and drink a cup of coffee.

* * * * * * *

Neesa woke up at 8:30 a.m. in her own bed sore, the pain medicine had worn off. She limped to the living room, saw her robe on the sofa and put it on. Her feet ached from working in stilettos all day yesterday and from stomping on the break to stop her car from going over the guardrail. The tiled floor soothed them, slightly. The old burns on her legs itched, she bent down to scratch and winced at the pain in her back.

Neesa took a glass from the wood dish rack and set it on the marble counter. Then poured a full glass of wine. *It was five o'clock somewhere,* she said to herself. She savored the crimson in her mouth and tightened the belt of her robe.

There was a draft coming from the open kitchen window. A window she did not remember opening. She walked over to it and peered out from the curtain. An uneasy feeling rushed through her battered body.

Am I being watched?

CHAPTER 13

Neesa

Neesa picked up the flyer that was on the table. She dropped it, startled by a knock on the door. It was too early for anyone to even think about coming to her place unannounced. She ignored the knocks, but they continued. Her senses heightened.

"I'm out front...open up.," yelled Chaz from the other side of the front door.

"Chaz?" answered Neesa.

"Yes, could you let me in?" he said.

She opened the door and gave him a questioning stare. He returned the stare with eyes of worry as he saw her bruised face.

She let tears flow from her eyes as she grieved Tracey.

"Neesa, what happened? I didn't get a text from you last night when you got home, and you did not answer your phone all morning." He made his way inside and followed her to the kitchen.

The two of them did not speak until after she poured him a glass of wine. She silently questioned her own life and why things were happening around and to her.

Her body ached. Her mind was unsettled with the bloody memory of Tracey and what came before and after it. Her thoughts must have shown on her face.

"Oh my God," said Chaz pulling her towards him. "What happened? Talk to me."

She told him about the car crash and her belief that it was an intentional hit.

"Nooooo, you can't be sure of that," he said reassuringly.

He grabbed her in his arms and held her tight. The belt of her robe had already come untied again and her naked body pressed against him. His hand cupped the back of her head and he pulled her in closer. Her arms wrapped around his neck, and she buried her face into it. He picked her up and she winced with pain as she wrapped her legs around him. Heat resonated between her opened legs. They made their way to the couch, both breathing deep sensual breaths. They looked at one another. Her hands unzipped him, and he stepped out of his jeans. He penetrated her hard and firm. Her nails dug into his back and grief ridden tears ran down her face. She let him out of the friendzone.

"Go deeper," she whispered in his ear. His buttocks tensed as he willed himself deeper inside. Her feline squeeze tight, barely registering his erection. The deep she needed, was too big of a request of him.

She let out a groan, which Chaz mistook as her climatic moan.

"I'm about to cum," he said.

"Not inside me." She jumped out of his arms and pushed him away.

He was barely able to stand as he released himself into his palm. Neesa was silent. Euphoria covered his face. He stared at her back as she walked away, unfulfilled.

She washed her hands in the kitchen sink and handed him a napkin. The sex did not quiet the misery in her mind. If anything, it added to the chaos.

Then she spoke.

"Chaz, I am in a whirlwind," she said. "Too much has happened this week and I can't keep up."

She looked down at the flyer resting atop a book on the kitchen table.

"Have you heard about this?" she said lifting it up so he could see it.

He walked over to her and read the lettering aloud "Come Unwind Your Mind."

"Never heard of it," he replied.

"It seems like the perfect place to runaway to," she said. "I need peace. I need time to regroup and figure out what is going on."

"Oh wow...Ummm...did you want some company?" he said.

She did not answer right away, instead she looked out the kitchen window and then back at the stove burner.

"I need to think," she said finally. "I want to go, right now. But I want to go alone."

"Are you sure that is smart," he said. "You shouldn't..."

"Don't tell me what I shouldn't do, Chaz," Neesa said. She snatched the flyer out of his hand. She saw his eyes darken and it sent chills through her body. He glared at her, went to snatch it back but then rescinded the action and held his hands at his waist in a controlled fist. Neesa, even though she was slightly alarmed, stepped to him because she was not going to back down to anyone in her own home.

Realizing he was fumbling in his new position, Chaz changed gears.

"I apologize," he said hoping she did not see the rage burning inside him. "I am just worried about you. Would you at least let me drive you up there? It's almost an hour a drive."

She did not answer right away.

* * * * * * * *

That evening, the two of them rode through the rain in silence. The two-lane freeway up the mountain was slippery as it was the first real rain of the season. The shoulder of the road was mostly flooded. She was beginning to regret her decision. Chaz was stoked to show off his new performance tread tires. His car hydroplaned and he maneuvered the car accordingly.

"Slow down Chaz," said Neesa.

"Sweetheart, I got this," said Chaz. "You do know, I come up here to go shooting at the range, right?"

"No, I never knew that. But I'm sure I don't know a lot about you," Neesa said.

"What's that supposed to mean?"

"One can never truly know anyone," she said. Thinking back to the words her ex had written before her world crumbled into shambles.

"Oh, you know me very well," he grinned as he took his hand off the clutch and squeezed her inner thigh. She pushed his hand away and told him to pay attention to the road. Chaz jerked his hand back to the steering wheel. He forced his car to slide left as the new tires fought hard to grip the slippery road where large rocks had fallen.

"Shit!" said Chaz.

A vehicle behind them had its high beams on and stayed close to the back of their car. Neesa looked back and a ball of nervousness gripped her.

"Chaz how long has that car been behind us?" she asked.

"Not long. It came out of nowhere," said Chaz. "I think it's a truck."

"It could be whoever was in my pad or who had killed Tracey or who had tried to kill me last night," said Neesa.

"I doubt it," said Chaz as he turned his car onto the dirt road which was supposed to lead up to the retreat. His car kicked up mud on the back window, making it difficult to see the vehicle behind them. The lights disappeared. They breathed a sigh of relief as they realized that the driver behind them must have turned off onto one of the side roads.

"See, I told you sweetheart," Chaz reassured Neesa. "Nothing to worry about. Just a local going home."

"Stop calling me sweetheart," she said. "I hate that name!"

Neesa's mind went back to the letter her ex had left her. How it was laced with the word *sweetheart.* He was a bastard. A manipulative monster.

Tension eased as the couple drove on. They talked about Tracey's murder and gossiped about the dancers at the club. The rain was coming down strong making it hard to see through the blurred watery curtain on the windshield.

Unease crept up Neesa's spine as she looked in the passenger side mirror. She saw a glimpse of something large in the glimmer of rain and moonlight. It was hard to tell what it was because the country road did not have streetlights.

Chaz kept chatting away.

"I knew you would have knocked Sonja on her ass," he said oblivious to Neesa's anxiousness. She remembered how her ex did not register her emotions either.

Suddenly, the car lurked forward and slid on the muddy clay. Something had rammed the car. Chaz tried to control his vehicle. A silhouette of a truck was behind them and picking up speed easily as its all-terrain tires gripped the ground. Chaz pressed his foot on the gas. The wheels of his car slid. Chaz made a sharp turn onto another dirt road. The silhouetted vehicle sped past them, spewing mud on their windshield.

"What the fuck is going on, Neesa?" asked Chaz. His pupils enlarged, beads of sweat formed on his forehead.

113

"How the hell am I supposed to know?" Neesa said.

"Sorry, sweetheart, I mean babe... this shit is crazy," he said. "We gotta call the cops."

"I am so sick of the police right now," she said looking up at the sign 'Shamba Place Bed and Breakfast.' "Pull in here," ordered Neesa. "I know where we're at."

Chaz did as he was instructed.

"Here? Where are we?" he asked.

"A bed and breakfast," she said.

"Are you getting romantic with me?" he teased, trying to calm her down.

"Shut up," she said, stretching the words out and rolling her eyes. Everything happens for a reason. But sometimes the reason is you are stupid and make bad decisions, she thought to herself.

CHAPTER 14

Janice

Rapid knocking on the door interrupted Janice while she was in the middle of writing a scene about a young couple driving out of town on a rainy night. She looked at the wall clock, it was a quarter past seven. Late for new arrivals.

The knocking got louder. The old woman set her pen and book on the table and walked to open the door. Janice stood shocked, speechless as she looked into the eyes of the young woman at the door.

Neesa was a perfect likeness to the woman Janice was writing about even though she had never drawn a picture of the character.

Then she spoke.

"Hi, I know it's late, but...," said the young woman as she offered her hand to Janice. "My name is Neesa, I spoke with you on the phone the other day."

Janice almost fell over on her wrinkled mahogany face.

"Neesa?" asked Janice.

There was an awkward pause. Janice had a look of bewilderment in her eyes. Neesa shared the same look of bewilderment even though she could not find a solid reason for the feeling.

"Ma'am can we come in?" interrupted Chaz. "We're soaked." He stretched out his arms to make a display of the obvious.

"Oh, sure, sure. Where are my manners? Welcome." Janice stepped aside, slightly bowed, and waved the couple in.

Janice let them stay at the ranch. She gave them the same tour she had given Micah and Cynthia. Neesa and Chaz went to their room, then Chaz went back downstairs. He asked Janice for a cup of tea for Neesa to help her sleep.

CHAPTER 15

Neesa

Chaz ended up staying the first night. As she stood sipping the warm tea, Neesa saw the agitation on his face when she pointed to the chair near the window.

"That's where you're sleeping," she said while sucking in her lips as they tingled from the tea herbs.

"C'mon, Neesa," he said stepping closer to her. "Let me hold you."

She to a step forward, keeping her finger pointed at the chair.

"Why are you getting all 'Jezebel' on me?" he said with an uncomfortable laugh.

Neesa said nothing, her look was enough. Chaz went to the seat and pulled the throw over him like a wounded dog.

* * * * * * *

As the golden hour ushered the morning in, Neesa sat up in bed and turned on the bedside lamp. Paper fell to the floor. She looked over to the window. The chair was empty. Her eyes surveyed the room. She was alone.

She then leaned over the bed and picked up the paper. There were two sheets folded together. She nestled back into the feathered pillow against the headboard. Her stomach began to turn as she read the word on the front. *Neesa.*

A lump formed in her throat. Memory of the letter her ex had left for her six months ago made it feel like spiders were running up her back. She held her breath and unfolded the pages.

Neesa, I like you so much. I would do anything for you.

Her eyes rolled in her head, and she exhaled a sigh of relief. *Just a love letter,* she thought.

She kept reading.

I know this sounds silly, but it's true. I feel so much when I'm with you. I didn't believe I could love someone so deeply, but here I am. We are meant for each other.

She shook her head side to side. They were obviously on two different pages. *Why did I have sex with him?* Uninterested in an outpour of unwelcomed affection, Neesa scanned over the first page of his note. Her eyes stopped at the last sentence.

Sweetheart, I just want to confess to you...

Sweat beaded on her nose, her head began to spin. Her fingers slid the second page up front.

A knock on the door startled her and she dropped the pages to the floor. Janice's voice was heard on the other side.

"When the leg does not walk, the stomach does not eat."

CHAPTER 16

Janice

Janice had to get another look at her new arrival. *Am I losing my mind?* she thought. The old woman snuck and listened at Neesa's door. It was quiet, however a dim light shone underneath the door.

The whole thing was strange. Janice did not know how or why, but she did know the woman behind the door. Something peculiar was going on and Janice had to get to the bottom of it. *Was it power? Was she crazy? Was it just a mere coincidence?*

"Breakfast is ready in thirty minutes," said Janice through the door.

"Thank you," said Neesa, her head was pounding. She realized she could not remember the last time she ate. "I'll be down."

Neesa left the fallen pages on the floor. She took a quick shower, brushed her teeth, and put on a long colorful dress she had packed. Her eyes darted down to Chaz's letter on the floor. She could not, she would not, read until she was ready. She picked it up, refolded it, and placed it on the nightstand.

His words echoed in her head: *Sweetheart, I just want to confess to you...*

CHAPTER 17

Neesa

"Oh, my god! Jezebel!" gasped Cynthia, then whispered. "Girl, I only know your stripper name. What are you doing here?"

"Hey, what's up," Neesa said through a forced smile. "My friends call me Neesa, you can call me Jezebel, though."

Cynthia did not pick up what Neesa had dropped. Cynthia spoke as though they were homegirls, which could not be further from the truth. She was one of the broads at the strip club who had laughed at Neesa's burns a few months back, on her first day of dancing. A week or so after that night, however, Cynthia was fired. She was not a high money maker.

Cynthia chatted away about how dusty and too country the B&B was for her. Her rambling was interrupted by a man who had walked up behind her. Neesa was caught off guard. She recognized Micah right away.

They stared at one another.

"Hey, Micah," Cynthia threaded her arm in his. "This is Jezebel...I mean Neesa."

"Hi," he said as recognition displayed on his face. "You two know each other?" he asked.

"Yeah, something like that," Neesa said as she made her plate. Janice had prepared eggs, bacon, veggie sausage, grits, fried apples, buttermilk biscuits, fresh fruit, rich coffee, and apple juice.

"Neesa, you can sit with Micah and me in the dining room," Cynthia offered.

"I was going to get some fresh air on the porch," she said. "Thanks though."

After breakfast, Janice made her way out to the porch to talk to her quiet new house guest.

"Where's that boy of yours?" asked Janice. "I haven't seen him today."

"He'll be back," Neesa said. "He had to go to work." She had not planned to have Chaz come back, but Janice did not need to know that. Neesa was conflicted with trust and distrust when it came to the woman. Her head was full of fuzz and confusion when she was around the older woman, however, her heart felt a kindred spirit.

Janice invited Neesa for a walk. At first, Neesa wanted to opt-out, but she thought she might come off as rude. She also needed to get some exercise and clear her head. What she had not expected was to completely pour her heart out and tell the old lady all of what had happened to her the past few days.

"I just can't believe Tracey was murdered," said Neesa. "I know it is my fault."

"Why would you think that?" asked Janice.

Neesa did not answer, and the two women continued to walk. Janice did not push her and that made Neesa more comfortable. She felt the urge to get things off her chest and for some reason Janice was easy to talk to. She was attentive and distant at the same time. She was there beside Neesa, listening but also inside her own mind, thinking.

Neesa began. "My boyfriend," she said. "My boyfriend," she said again.

"Take your time *sweetheart*," said Janice.

"Why'd you call me that?" Neesa said sharply.

"I didn't mean anything by it, child. Old folk speech." Janice fluttered her hand to signal Neesa to continue. "Get your panties out your ass."

Neesa was taken aback at the old woman's response, then she smiled. It was nice to hear someone keep it real.

"My ex-boyfriend murdered people," Neesa blurted out.

Janice looked unphased, so Neesa closed her eyes and spoke.

"Then he killed himself in the garage, suicide by carbon monoxide."

She opened her eyes and Janice was looking deep into them.

"There was an explosion, and I was left with these," she said lifting her dress to show Janice the scars going up both legs.

Janice looked down but remained quiet. Neesa thought she may have frightened the older woman. She let go of her dress, the hem slid to her ankles.

"Damnit, I said too much," she said out loud while silently chastising herself for opening up.

"That is some crazy shit." Janice finally said. "How did you find out what he had done?"

"He left me a fucking letter," said Neesa, looking far off at nothing.

129

Remembering the day, she walked into the kitchen and saw the envelope and journal on the kitchen table.

Neesa looked off into the distance.

Janice rubbed her own temples. *Was this a game? Who could have put her up to it though?*

"I am not sure what to do at this point," Neesa said.

"He who does not know one thing, knows another," said Janice. She turned and headed back to the house.

Neesa was perplexed but shook it off. She enjoyed the solitude outside amongst the trees. Her sorrow darkened. Anger and curiosity stirred within her. She was going to find the underlying cause of all of it. She just was unsure where to begin.

Neesa strolled along the mud path, thinking about the disheveled puzzle called her life. The rays of sunlight that seeped from behind the clouds felt good. She looked for a dry spot to sit, since the ground was still wet from the previous night's rain. As she scanned her surroundings, she realized she was near an old barn. It needed a paint job. Compared to the main house, the barn was a misfit. The chipped red paint had a weathered brown tint. Boarded windows made it look like an abandoned farmhouse. She walked towards it and noticed a drop in the temperature. Something about the place made her want to look inside. The front door was locked, and the front window was painted black. She went around back and noticed some double barn doors which had a lock on them as well. The place looked like no one ever came out to it. What caught her eyes were fresh footprints that led up to the barn doors and continued underneath, inside. Eventually, she found a window without boards. It had been painted black just like the front window but there was a small, uncovered section in the bottom corner. Neesa needed something to stand on so she could peer through the old window.

Looking around the outside, Neesa found a petrified log and scooted the piece of wood, under the window, held onto the chipped window seal, and stepped up. It wobbled on the soft mud.

131

The barn was empty for the most part. Yet, the place did not look abandoned. Someone went there often. It had a weird organization about it, as though someone was living in the place. There was a sink on the far wall with a ragged towel hung on it. There appeared to be a bed, but Neesa was not sure. Something else was there. Something large and covered. Neesa thought it may have been a tractor but then again, a tractor *was too large. An antique* car she thought as she looked a little harder. Large tires sat below the tarp.

"Can I help you with something?" asked Janice. The older woman's voice startled Neesa causing her to stumble off the log.

"No. I was just about to go up to the house," said Neesa.

"Did you hurt yourself?" Janice said more accusatory than caring.

Neesa shook her head no.

"I want to make sure my guests are okay."

"I'm fine," said Neesa as she brushed mud off her dress and walked past the old woman. She could feel the hard glare Janice was giving her. Goosebumps rose on Neesa's arms and neck.

"This barn is my husband Jack's. No one is allowed here but him!" said Janice. "If you do need anything it would serve you better to ask rather than snoop!"

Neesa walked away, hastily.

Neesa could not brush the uneasy feeling she had when it came to Shamba Place and Janice. It felt as though the old woman was always looking at her. One thing she knew for sure was when everyone was asleep, she would give the barn another visit.

****

Upstairs in her room, the old woman sat on her bed in deep thought. She was ready for Micah and Cynthia to leave. She wanted to put her whole focus on Neesa.

She picked up her writing material, the corners of her lips rose, she knew what she had to do.

A fight between grasshoppers is a joy to the crow.

133

CHAPTER 18

Micah

"I hate it here," said Cynthia. "I am so ready to leave."

"That's great, Cynthia," said Micah.

"What is so great about it?" she asked as she flicked ashes out the window.

"You're leaving," he said.

"What are you talking about?" asked Cynthia. "We're leaving, now?" Her faced brightened.

Micah kicked Cynthia's bags towards the door. "I'll help you take these down. I called a cab," he said to her.

It took a minute; her eyes went from her bags to him.

"Who the hell do you think you are?" Cynthia said in surprise. "You can't just kick me out, you brought me up here."

"I realized what a mistake that was," he said. "Don't get me wrong, it was good, until it wasn't." Micah was blunt with Cynthia. He knew the only way he would get rid of her was to take her by surprise. He also wanted to free himself up for Neesa. It had to be more than a coincidence that they were both there at the old bed and breakfast at the same time. He felt ashamed about dissing her the other night.

"Oh, I see. You want that dumb broad, Jezebel!" said Cynthia.

Neesa

Down the hall, Neesa rolled her eyes as she overheard Micah and Cynthia arguing. *Cynthia is an idiot. Why was she even fighting the situation? Micah could not have been more direct.*

Janice

Janice smiled as she slid on her shoes and walked downstairs. The couple was still arguing when they arrived at the bottom. She sat her journal down on the table at the front entry way and began to bark orders.

"Get her out of here, right now!" Janice said.

Cynthia stuck her middle finger up at Janice. Janice stepped forward; eyes filled with fury.

The force of the smack across her face caused Cynthia to stumble backwards knocking Janice's journal to the ground. She screamed and touched her mouth. Blood dripped from her split lip.

"I'll sue you," she said. "I'll take everything you have, you old bitch!"

"Cynthia, let's go!" Micah took hold of her elbow and her bags. Janice stood on the porch steps, not blinking. *It worked*, she thought to herself. *It worked!* Her wrinkled lips rose in a smile.

Neesa

Neesa had come out of her room just as Janice had reached the bottom. She watched the arguing in amusement. She saw the tilted table leaning against the wall. Her eyes looked down. A book was sprawled open on the floor. Its leather cover turned upward. It resembled *his* book. The one from her ex. She hesitated, held her breath and then picked it up. She flipped it open to the bookmarked place and the title of the page read Neesa. Her mind began to blur, her head spun, and she was jerked forward, her hands extended in front of her.

Janice

"Give me that," Janice said as she snatched it out of Neesa's hands and hugged the book close to her old breasts.

"My bad, I found it laying on the ground," said Neesa.

"Sure, you did," Janice said stuffing the journal in her bosom. It stuck out

awkwardly underneath the top of her kaftan
as the only two suckas she could trust kept
her written words safe from prying eyes.

CHAPTER 19

Janice

Night came quickly, and Janice was ready for bed. She recalled how brash she had spoken to Neesa throughout the day, but the remorse was short-lived. She couldn't care less about Neesa's feelings. The young woman was not real. How could she be? The thought brought out a wet laugh from the old woman's dry lips.

But, if she was not real, does that make me a lunatic? No, Neesa was a real breathing being. Right?

Janice believed Neesa had seen what was written in the book. If that had happened, then Neesa knew too much. Janice was unsure of what that meant for herself. Would she be sent to jail or a mental institution? On the other hand, Janice knew the story was too farfetched for anyone to believe.

Janice devised a plan to get rid of Neesa. She would write the young woman out of the story. She toyed with different ideas in her head. She could write a scene where Neesa hung herself in her room. *It would be believable* since she seemed depressed anyway. She could make a scene where Neesa choked on a piece of food, and no one was able to revive her. *No,* she thought. *That would not work.* What if Micah knew CPR?

She decided she would wait until she had a great plan before she killed off her main character. For now, she decided to have a little fun and see just how attached Neesa was to the tip of her pen.

The old woman went to the last marked place in the book, flipped to a fresh page and began to draft a new story about her lead character.

Neesa

Neesa sat up in bed and pulled back the blanket from her naked body. She stared at her bedroom door then laid back down and pulled the blanket back up. She was restless, her legs itched. She got out of bed, her body was heavy, and she moved about her room in an ethereal state. Her soft hands smoothed shea butter over her scars. She looked at her hands, and then thought about *his* hands. Micah's large strong hands.

She sat on the chair of the aged, white vanity alongside the wall and traced dark plum lipstick over her full lips. She put on a nightshirt. Then stared into the mirror mesmerized by something and nothing at the same time.

Her hand slid between her inner thighs and warmed themselves between her moist fold. Her forehead was wet with perspiration, and she was in need.

* * * * * * * *

Janice turned the page and continued writing.

Neesa

Neesa got up and walked to the door, her hand was sticky with her creamy flow as she turned the doorknob. The hallway was quiet. She walked down to Micah's door and knocked lightly.

Her need deepened. She throbbed inside.

There was movement inside the room. Micah opened the door in boxer briefs. His body was radiating sex. He smelled magnificent.

"Neesa, right?" He asked. "What's up?"

She saw the way he took in her body and scent and watched as he became erect.

"Hello," he said licking his lips. His eyes deep in hers.

* * * * * * * *

Down the hall, in her own room, Janice's head dropped to her chest; heavy breath came from her lips. The tired old woman fell asleep, mid-sentence. Her journal sprawled in her lap.

* * * * * * *

Neesa blinked, her breasts were tender, her nipples were showing through her night shirt. She crossed her arms over her chest in embarrassment.

Micah blinked and placed his large hand over the front of his pants to hide his erection. Embarrassment flooded his face.

"Oh my god! My bad," said Neesa as she turned on her bare heels and rushed away, embarrassed and confused. She felt his stare on her for a few seconds and then heard his door close.

CHAPTER 20

Neesa

It was ten-past midnight, she could not shake the weird feeling she just had. *Why did she go to Micah's room?*

She had been at *Shamba Place* a full day. Neesa tried to sleep with no avail. She decided to go for a night walk and check out the barn, again. She put on the same dress she had been wearing that day and then looked to the nightstand beside her bed. Chaz's letter was still there, waiting for her to finish reading it. She picked it up, crumbled it in her hands, and shoved the papers in her dress pocket. She was still not ready.

The sharp edges of the crumpled letter scratched her skin beneath the dress. She put her hand in her pocket and smushed the letter flat against her body.

The chill from the air was softened by the warmth of her breath. She used the flashlight of her cell phone to guide her down the path.

It was dark, she could barely see her hand outstretched in front of her. Crickets chirped. She heard tiny rustles around her. Something ran over her foot causing her to jump. She took a deep breath, trying to keep her composure. Neesa looked up at the trees that towered above. Shadows that spread across the road tried to stop her from continuing her journey. She sucked it up and continued walking. There were more pressing issues. *Who is after me?* Neesa was sure the answers to at least one of her questions was in the barn. *Who was Janice?*

Something ran across her path. It was a large rat. She heard a rustle in bushes near her. Neesa stopped and put her cell in her pocket. Suddenly, fear flooded her body. *Is there a coyote or mountain lion watching me out here?* She could see the outline of the barn up ahead. There was no turning back. Neesa shook the thoughts of animals attacking her and tearing her to shreds. She kept walking. She remembered an old saying, *'Restless feet might walk you in a snake pit.'*

She reached the barn and stepped up on the same log as earlier to look through the window. It was difficult to see at anything at night. It was dark in the old shack. She walked around to the back of the barn, found the door, and turned the cold knob. She was sure it would be locked. Neesa tried it anyway and the barn door creaked open. A rush of funky air slapped Neesa in the face and rushed outside behind her. The aged stench nearly knocked her over. The smell was intense. Thick; a mixture of a dead rat and some other rotting animal. She felt transported back to Tracey's house. Her skin prickled with fear, but she pushed on. Her inner voice reminded her, *Tracey was not there, this was a different place. A different situation.*

The place needed to be aired out. Bile rose to the center of Neesa's throat. She swallowed the acid back down.

As she stepped into the barn, she closed the door behind her. She slowed her breathing. The funk of the place was distracting. She crept further inside, kicking a bucket as she did. It rolled across the dirt floor. She took out her cellphone again and used its flashlight. She walked to the tarp she had seen covering a vehicle earlier. She looked down at the tires. The stench was strong where Neesa stood.

She put her phone in her pocket and gently pulled at the tarp. Everything came to her all at once. The muddy tires. The dark paint. The dusty truck. There was something leaning forward inside. Without thinking, she reached into the open window and tried to lift whatever it was up. Her hands sunk into hollows of skin, dry cloth, and bone. She pulled her hands out and looked at them. They were sticky with a gelatin substance and gritty bits. She held back a scream and readjusted her eyes. She wiped her hands on her dress and pulled her phone out of her pocket. Her cellphone illuminated; a body slumped over the steering wheel. It had been there for quite some time.

Neesa ran out of the barn, tripping over the bucket as she fled. Her stomach unleashed a vile mass of emotion in the form of acidic milk chunks. She threw up until she was dry heaving. She could not figure out why awful things were happening around her. *What the hell is going on!? Who is Janice? Who is dead in that truck? Why?* She breathed through each thought and quieted them. After she got herself back together, Neesa rushed back to the main house.

She needed to get off the ranch, *but how?* She was alone without a car. She remembered the notebook Janice had snatched from her hands earlier. Neesa needed to see what was inside; perhaps all of the answers she was looking for."

Her thoughts went to Micah. *He* could help me.

Micah

"Micah," whispered Neesa as she knocked softly. The lights were off in his room. She hoped he could hear her. She did not want to raise her voice and wake up Janice.

At first, he thought he was dreaming. Micah could hear her voice in his head, calling him. It was a soft tone, sweet. He rubbed himself and began to harden in his palm.

There was a loud knock on the door. His eyes

opened.

Damnit, he thought. Just when the dream was getting good.

He jumped out of bed, wrapped a sheet around his waist and opened the door.

"Hey," he said. "What's up?"

Neesa pushed past him. He followed her with his eyes, slowly shut his door, and waited. Something was wrong. Her warm brown skin had paled. Terror was written on her face.

"I need your help," she said. "First, how well do you know Janice?"

"Since I was young. Everybody out here knows pretty much everyone. Other than that, she was just a neighbor. Why? What's up?" he asked again.

"I need to show you something outside," she said.

"Right, now?" Micah asked. Of course, he thought she was attractive, however, currently she was disheveled, uneasy. Her hair was a mess, sweat beaded her brow. She was trembling. She smelled of rot.

His dick went soft.

Neesa grabbed his grey sweats off the floor and tossed them his way. "Let's go. I don't feel comfortable talking here."

As they neared the barn, the rancid air cooled. Neesa took out her cell phone for light. Micah held his pocket flashlight in his hand.

153

"Did you bring me out here to take pictures?" he joked. He knew something serious was going on, but he wanted to lighten the mood.

"Wait until you see what is inside, then you'll know why," she said to him.

They went in and Neesa immediately regretted coming back to the barn and started to second guess herself. *What if Micah was in on everything with Janice?* she thought. That was a risk she had to take. She needed his help.

Micah remembered this place. He had been there when he was young. He would come down to the ranch with his mother to pick oranges. His trips to the ranch stopped when his mother left the family.

"Smells like...a dead rat," Micah said as he covered his nose and mouth with his inner elbow. "Or a dead horse."

"Come over here and I'll show you," Neesa said trembling as she took Micah's hand and guided him through the dark. She stopped at the uncovered truck. She was afraid. She was worried there would be nothing there and Micah would think she was a fool.

"Look!" She guided him to the truck and turned away. Micah stepped in front of the car and peered in.

"What the hell?" he said, jumping back, almost dropping his flashlight. "What the hell is going on?"

"Who is that...?" he looked closer. "Is that her husband?"

Neesa was shaking all over, hardly able to speak. "I think so. Janice must have done this, I know it."

Micah reached into the truck, Neesa grabbed his arm.

"What are you doing?" she asked.

He ignored her question as he looked at a jasper pendent hanging from the rearview mirror. He yanked it free and put it in his pocket.

"Why would Janice kill her husband?" Micah asked, even though he seemed miles away. "Are you sure?"

Micah wondered if he should trust Neesa. She had been off beat since she arrived and now this. He was not sure, but deep in his gut he knew he had to help her.

"I don't have proof but let's go outside," she said. "I can't stay in here." When they were out of the barn Micah asked Neesa again how she was sure that Janice was responsible for the corpse inside.

"Something just seemed strange about her. Did you see the way she acted earlier when I picked her book off the floor? She practically ripped my arm off when she snatched it out of my hands," she said.

"Also, I haven't seen her husband since I've been here. Have you?

He shook his head no.

"That was crazy," he said. "I thought it was a lady diary or something like that."

He thought back.

"When Cynthia and I arrived up here, Janice acted as though we were strangers. I just figured she didn't recognize me because it had been several years since I've been back," he said.

Neesa shrugged.

"I need to get out of here," she said. "I need a ride and you are going to help me."

"Let's go get our bags and bounce," he said.

"I want to get that book of hers first," she said.

"You want a book?" One of his eyebrows lifted. He was rethinking his new alliance.

"I have a feeling there is something important in it," said Neesa. "She's sleeping right now, though."

"I know how to wake her," Micah said as he took a lighter out of his pocket. "I'll start a small fire, put it out, then go to her room and tell her there was a fire. She will run to the barn. That will give you enough time to go to her room and get the book."

"Meet me on the side of the house by my car," he said.

"We can't let the body burn, it's evidence. Can you help me move him," Neesa asked? She felt insane. She had just convinced herself to move a decomposing body.

Micah put his hand on her shoulder. "I'll take care of it. Go to the house. Now!" he said. Before she could argue with him, he was back inside.

Adrenaline was racing through her veins. She ran, fast. Sliding on mud, but not falling.

Micah found a crumbled newspaper and a gas can in the barn. He splashed gas onto a log leaning inside the barn, careful not to get any on himself. He lit the paper. Flames burst up. The smell was earthy. He waited a few minutes until he was sure Neesa had had enough time to get back in the house, then threw dirt and mud on the flames. Smoke filled the barn. The log was still hot and red underneath the soil.

He ran up to the house to wake Janice.

CHAPTER 21

Neesa

Back in her guest room, Neesa heard Micah bang on the old woman's door. There was a commotion and loud voices. Footsteps rushed down the stairs. A door slammed shut. The house was quiet.

Neesa snuck out of her room and crept into Janice's large bedroom. The space smelled of must, perfume, and sour feet. It was foul. There was no time to think about the funk. She had to find the notebook. She looked at the nightstand, which was a logical place. The book was not there. She looked to the floor and saw it. The pen was beside it.

The journal had fallen off the nightstand when Janice rushed out of bed.

Neesa sat on the bed and flipped open the cover. The first couple pages were blank. The first page with words read "Jack." She skimmed through it.

Jack came into the kitchen from the back door. I sat at the kitchen table reading his notebook. Then, I turned around startled. I knew he could see my fear. I stood up and backed away. He darted towards me. I tried to run away, but he grabbed my hair as I screamed and tried to break free. A powerful blow to my temple caused me to blackout for a minute. When I came to, his hands were around my neck squeezing tight. I did not fight back.

He dropped me to the floor.

"Now look what you made me do. Get up, woman!" Jack said. "You hear me?"

I remained motionless. He thought he killed me. Then he walked across the house aimlessly trying to figure out what to do next. He was annoyed and blamed me for dying. He cursed me then wrapped my body

*in a blanket and carried it to his truck. He
dropped my body across the passenger side
seat. My head fell to the driver's seat. He
hopped in on the driver's side and pushed
my head over with his hip as he squeezed
into the front cab. He drove down and
parked near his old barn and took me out of
the truck.*

*As he carried my limp body, he
paused. I think he felt me move. He dropped
me down to the ground and went into the
barn to get a shovel. Then, he came back
outside.*

My body was gone.

Neesa flipped through more of the
pages and read that Janice had pretended to
be dead, then snuck away when Jack left to
get his shovel.

Neesa's head rose as she heard Janice
yelling at Micah from outside. She kept
reading.

*There was a two-by-four in the back
of the truck. I took it and hid in the shadows.
When he was close enough, I jumped out*

ready to smash his brains in. He tripped and hit his head on a tree root, instead.

He looked unconscious but I was not convinced so I hit him in the head just to be sure.

When he came to, he was sitting in his truck. Right where he had thrown my body. It was hard lifting his heavy ass up in that damn thing. I tied his hands and feet and stuffed his mouth with dirt. He tried to wiggle free, but the rope did not give. He began to gag as he spat mud at me.

Neesa continued to skip through more pages.

Janice wrote that she had opened the double barn doors and backed the truck inside. Jack continued to struggle for freedom. Janice jumped out the truck, leaving the exhaust on and ran out of the barn covering her nose and mouth. She shut the doors and shoveled mud to seal the opening underneath.

I let the exhaust fumes send Jack to hell.

That is what Janice meant earlier about Jack being the only one allowed at the barn. He was still there, dead. Murdered. Janice killed her husband and wrote about it.

As Neesa skipped through more pages, she came upon the recent entries. The hair on the back of her neck began to stand up. It could not be true, but it was plain as day.

Neesa was reading, reliving her own story. It was all in there, the gas leak, Tracey's murder, her car accident. She tried to look away, but she could not take her eyes away from the pages. She finally felt vindicated, she was right. Something was not right with the old woman. Something was not right with her *own* life.

But how? How did Janice know all these things? There were still details missing. Who killed Tracey? Who turned her stove on? Who drove her off the road? The scenes were laid out in precision; however, the culprit was still masked. Did Janice know who it was?

Neesa was furious and did not understand how the old woman had portions of her life written in that book. All the journal entries were dated before Neesa had even arrived at Shamba Place, except for two: when Cynthia had left and when Neesa had gone to Micah's room in a daze.

She stuffed the journal in one of her dress side pockets and rushed out of the house to find Micah.

Janice

"What happened out here?" demanded Janice as she and Micah stood at the entrance of the smokey barn.

"I'm not sure. I was looking out the window when I saw smoke. That is when I came to get you," Micah lied.

"I can handle it from here." Janice waved him off.

Micah ignored her and walked several steps into the dark barn. The air was rancid. Janice grabbed his arm. He shook her bony fingers off and moved further inside. She followed him.

"Get out of here!" said Janice, her voice wavered slightly. "I told you, I can handle it."

She heard a noise and turned toward the door.

"For crying out loud!" Janice saw Neesa's silhouetted frame in the entrance. "What are you doing out here?!" she said to Neesa.

"I heard the noise and came down," said Neesa. "What happened?"

"A damn fire, girl," snapped Janice. "You both can go!"

"Ma'am, I just want to look around and make sure it's safe for you," he squinted in the darkness. He covered his nose with the inside of his elbow.

Neesa walked inside, unable to fully see. Janice grabbed Micah with more power in her grip and yanked him towards the exit. Micah, surprised by the force, stumbled into Neesa. She in turn, almost lost her footing, nearly falling to the floor. Her dress caught the corner of a makeshift counter and ripped.

There was a thud, then a louder one, then two.

"Get your hands off me," Neesa said to Janice.

She stomped repeatedly. Janice's fear of her husband's dead body being discovered, turned to rage.

"Get out of here," she said. "Now!"

"Fine, fine," Micah said, his hands raised in surrender.

Micah and Neesa stood outside. He yelled to Janice.

"You want me to call the fire department or sheriff?"

"No!" she said.

"Go, go...get out of here!" Janice shooed them away and went inside the barn. The barn was smokey. Her eyes had already adjusted to the darkness, but the sting of the smoke blurred her vision.

Janice sensed from the first time she had laid eyes on Neesa that trouble was brewing. Suddenly it seemed her world was tumbling down. She had to move quickly to get things out of the barn before morning. She hoped Micah and Neesa would mind their business until then.

Carefully walking through the dark, Janice made her way to where the truck was supposed to be. She had to get rid of Jack.

Fumes from smoke were taking its toll on her lungs. Janice's head began to spin. She sensed she was being watched.

I must get out of here, she thought. Her hands fumbled the pockets of her kaftan. *Where is my journal? Where is it?* In her haste to get down to the burning barn, she had left it in her room.

She needed her journal. She needed to write herself out of this situation.

She began to cough; her throat was dry. The smoke thickened.

The air should have cleared by now, she thought. Unbeknownst to her, the log Micah had set fire to and then covered with dirt began to rekindle.

She started choking. Wheezing on her hands and knees, Janice crawled on the floor. Fumes began to replace the air in her lungs. She leaned against the truck and peered through the smoke. A slither of moonlight peaked through the open barn door. In the moon's spotlight she saw it. Her journal, on the floor. *Can't be, she thought. Must be a mirage?*

She cursed, then cried out, as she tried to *will* her journal over to herself. A flame touched the leather, and it began to smolder.

"Ouch," Neesa said rubbing her arm. She was standing outside the barn, waiting for Janice to come out.

"What the hell?" said Micah as he hopped from one foot to the other. They looked at one another in dismay. She was hot, overly hot. She touched her arm. Her skin was wet. Then she noticed her skin searing as blood trickled down her nose. She smelled scorched flesh.

Micah's shirt began to burn.

Neesa felt for the journal that was supposed to be in her dress pocket.

"The journal!" she yelled. "I have to go back in there and get her journal." Her throat was dry and acidic fluid began to well up.

"Neesa, no," said Micah as he fell to the ground. His pants were in flames. Bright red peeked through burnt flesh.

She could not hear him, the pain in her body was too intense. She began to run to the barn. Her feet were hot; her face was steaming. She covered her nose and mouth with her shirt, held her breath and darted into the burning barn. She got on her knees and crawled. She swept her hands along the floor to feel for Janice's journal. She bumped its leather cover, and then her body jerked backward.

Something had a hold of her ankle. She tried to shake free while peering back through the smoke down her leg. Janice was still alive, and her wiry hand had a death grip on Neesa's leg.

Neesa shook her leg frantically to separate herself from the old woman. Chaz's crumbled letter fell from Neesa's dress pocket.

"Give me my journal," said Janice. Her vocals were the sound of fingernails scratching a chalkboard.

Neesa kicked free, slamming the heel of her foot into Janice's face. Bone crunched on impact, and Janice's grip loosened. She kicked at the old woman's head once more to make sure she was no longer a problem. Neesa lifted herself up to a standing position, grabbed the journal, and buried it in her own bosom.

Neesa's lungs were tight and would not expand. Her throat let out a dry cough. She could hear the gargled blood breaths of the old woman.

Neesa gasped for air, her legs buckled, and her body fell to the floor.

Micah appeared in the barn, lifted Neesa into his arms, and ran out the barn. Just then something struck him on the back of the head. He dropped Neesa in the dirt.

Turning around to see what hit him, he raised his arm just as Chaz swung a shovel at him.

"I'm going to kill you too," Chaz said to Micah.

Micah grabbed the shovel mid-swing. The men struggled; Micah pushed Chaz closer to the barn. Micah yanked the shovel out of Chaz's hand and used it to strike an upward blow on Chaz's chin. Chaz's feet fumbled underneath, carrying him closer to the flames of the barn. Blood sprayed out his mouth as he tripped on a log. His head went through one of the painted barn windows. The glass impelled him. His body seized for several seconds; then he went motionless.

"Is he dead?" Neesa got up and stood next to Micah. He dropped the shovel and put his arm around her shoulder.

Neesa shuddered.

Janice's high-pitched screams pierced the air. She was not dead; she must have only passed out from Neesa's kick.

Janice held on to life as the fire scorched her back. She held on even as her flesh burned from her body. She held on as the heat crawled down her throat and seared her lungs. Her scream bellowed loudly breaking the barn windows.

Then her story came to its end.

CHAPTER 22

Neesa

A year later, Neesa found herself sitting on her porch, in a new city. She had moved, again, after finding out from a detective that Chaz was responsible for murdering Tracey. Neesa never ended up reading the last page of his letter.

She thought about Micah. After everything had happened, he had told her that he realized Jack (Janice's husband) was responsible for his mother's disappearance when he saw his mother's necklace hanging on the mirror in the abandoned barn truck. He also told Neesa he had left Jack's body in the truck to burn. Experiences like theirs could either bring people closer or tear them apart.

For them it was the latter.

She looked down at her hands, holding Janice's journal in her lap.

"Can characters ever be released from their story?" she asked softly.

A warm wisp air touched her ear. She heard a whisper.

By the time the fool has learned the game, the players have dispersed.

Neesa held the tip of her pen to the page and took a deep breath.

About the Author

M. Woodard-Baylor was born on the East Coast and raised in Southern California. She earned a Master of Arts degree in strategic communication, is a PhD candidate and has a love for writing fiction, specifically mystery/suspense. In her free time, she enjoys going to the beach, roller-skating, reading, spending time with family, and creating stories. She is a mother, entrepreneur, and teacher.

Made in the USA
Las Vegas, NV
03 January 2022